THE FORCE IS WITH THEM . . .

JACEN loves living things. He keeps pets of all species: animals, plants, insects (some easier to care for than others . . .) and he suspects he can speak to them using the Force . . . though he doesn't quite know how.

JAINA takes after her father, Han. She is a mechanical whiz, always dismantling droids, machines, anything she can get her hands on. Like Han, her spirit and self-confidence sometimes get her into trouble.

LOWBACCA, or "Lowie," is the Wookiee nephew of Chewbacca and a native of the planet Kashyyyk. Taller than any of the others, he loves to climb to the top of Yavin 4's massive jungle trees. And on his belt, he wears . . .

EM TEEDEE, a translator droid built by Chewbacca to convert Wookiee speech to Basic. But because Em Teedee was programmed by See-Threepio, he tends to talk more than he has to.

TENEL KA is the tough, self-sufficient daughter of Teneniel Djo, one of the witches of Dathomir. Loyal, though a little humorless, she will fight beside her friends whenever they find themselves in tough situations.

This book also contains
a special sneak preview of the next *Star Wars: Young Jedi Knights* adventure:

THE LOST ONES

STAR WARS
YOUNG JEDI KNIGHTS
SHADOW ACADEMY

KEVIN J. ANDERSON
and REBECCA MOESTA

BOULEVARD BOOKS, NEW YORK

STAR WARS: YOUNG JEDI KNIGHTS
SHADOW ACADEMY

A Boulevard Book / published by arrangement with
Lucasfilm Ltd.

PRINTING HISTORY
Boulevard edition / September 1995

ISBN: 1-57297-025-1

BOULEVARD
Boulevard Books are published by The Berkley Publishing Group,
200 Madison Avenue, New York, New York 10016.
BOULEVARD and the "B" design
are trademarks belonging to The Berkley Publishing Corporation.

PRINTED IN THE UNITED STATES OF AMERICA

10 9 8 7 6 5 4 3 2 1

To our brothers and sisters—

Mark—who has been my hero since childhood. A true Jedi Knight, always ready to race to the rescue

Cindy—who always watched out for me. You showed me that effort and determination will get you what wishing and waiting will not

Diane—who broadened my horizons. Thanks for forcing me to watch every monster-and-hero movie ever made

Scott—who tolerated all the books I read to him. Thanks for telling me in May of 1977 that there was a movie I just had to go see—*Star Wars*

Rebecca Moesta

and *Laura*—for never fighting with me, always understanding (just kidding!), and providing a wealth of experiences for me to draw upon in my writing

Kevin J. Anderson

acknowledgments

We would like to thank Lil Mitchell for her tireless typing and for urging us to bring her each chapter faster and faster, Dave Wolverton for his input on Dathomir, Lucy Wilson and Sue Rostoni at Lucasfilm for their unwavering support, Ginjer Buchanan and Lou Aronica at Berkley/Boulevard for their continuing enthusiasm, Jonathan MacGregor Cowan for being our test audience . . . and Skip Shayotovich, Roland Zarate, Gregory McNamee, and the entire *Star Wars* ImagiNet Echo computer bulletin board for helping out with the jokes.

STAR WARS

YOUNG JEDI KNIGHTS

WARS.

SHADOW ACADEMY

JACEN GRASPED THE lightsaber, feeling its comforting weight against his sweaty palms. His scalp tingled beneath its unruly tangle of brown curls as he sensed the approach of his enemy. Closer, closer . . . He drew in a slow breath and reached with one finger that trembled ever so slightly to press the button on the handle.

With a buzzing hiss, the cold metal handle sprang to life, transforming into a sword of glowing energy. The deadly lightsaber pulsed and vibrated in his hands like a living thing.

With a mixture of fear and excitement, Jacen's wiry frame tensed for the attack. His liquid-brown eyes fluttered shut for a moment as he visualized his opponent.

Without warning, he heard the hum of a lightsaber slice down from above.

Jacen whirled just in time and caught the blow with his own lightsaber. The deep red of his opponent's weapon throbbed with power, filling his vision as the two glowing blades warred for dominance.

Jacen knew he was far outmatched in size and strength, that he would need all of his wits to get out of this encounter alive. His arms ached with the strain of holding off the blow, so he took advantage of his smaller size, spinning under his opponent's arm and dancing out of reach.

The attacker advanced toward him, but Jacen knew better than to let him get that close again. The ruby glow flashed toward him, and he was ready. He parried the blow and then swept sideways with his own blade before dodging backward and blocking the next thrust.

Attack and counterattack. Thrust. Parry. Block. Lightsabers sizzled and hissed as they clashed again and again.

Though the room was cool and dank, perspiration ran down Jacen's face and into his eyes, nearly blinding him. He saw the arc of red light barely in time and ducked to avoid it. A cocky lopsided grin sprang to his lips, and he realized he was enjoying himself. Stone chips flew around him as the deadly ruby blade gouged the low ceiling just over his head.

Jacen's grin faded as he tried to take a step backward and felt cold stone blocks press into his shoulder blades. He parried another thrust, sprang sideways, and fetched up against another stone wall.

He was cornered. An icy fist of fear clenched his

stomach, and Jacen dropped to one knee, flinging up his blade to ward off the next blow. A sound like thunder echoed through the chamber. . . ,

Jacen opened his eyes and looked up to see his uncle Luke standing in the doorway, clearing his throat. Startled, Jacen fumbled to turn off the lightsaber and accidentally dropped the extinguished handle to the flagstones with a clatter.

The sandy-haired, black-robed Jedi Master strode into the private room that served as both his office and his meditation chamber at the Jedi academy. He held his hand out toward the lightsaber, and the weapon sprang to his palm as if magnetized.

Jacen gulped as Master Luke Skywalker fixed him with a solemn gaze. "I'm sorry, Uncle Luke," Jacen said, his words coming out in a tumbling rush. "I came here to ask you for your help, and when you weren't here, I decided to wait, and then I saw your lightsaber just lying on your desk, and I know you said I'm not ready yet, but I didn't see how it could hurt to just practice a little. So I picked it up, and I guess I just got carried away and—"

Luke held up one hand, palm outward, as if to forestall further explanation. "The weapon of the Jedi shouldn't be taken up lightly," he said.

Jacen felt his cheeks flush at the gentle rebuke. "But I *know* I could learn to use a lightsaber," he said, defensive. "I'm old enough, and I'm tall enough, and I've been practicing in my room with a piece of pipe I got from Jaina—I'm sure I could do it."

Luke seemed to consider this for a moment before shaking his head slowly. "There'll be time enough for that when you are ready."

"But I'm ready *now*," Jacen protested.

"Not yet," Luke said, smiling sadly. "The time will come soon enough."

Jacen groaned with impatience. It was always *Later*, always *Some other time*, always *Maybe when you're older*. He sighed. "You're the teacher. I'm the student, so I have to listen, I guess."

Luke smiled and shook his head. "Ah. Be careful—don't assume a teacher is always right, without question. You have to think for yourself. Sometimes we teachers make mistakes, too. But in this case, I am right: You're not yet ready for a lightsaber.

"Believe me, I know what it's like to wait," Luke continued. "But patience can be as strong an ally as any weapon." Then his eyes twinkled. "Don't you have more important things to be worrying about right now than imaginary lightsaber battles—like getting ready for your trip? Don't your pets need to be fed?"

"I'm all packed, and I'll feed the animals just before we leave," Jacen said, thinking of the menagerie of pets he had collected since coming to the jungle moon. "But the trip *is* what I came here to talk to you about."

Luke raised his eyebrows. "Yes?"

"I—I was hoping you could talk to Tenel Ka and convince her to come with us to see Lando Calrissian's mining station."

Luke's brows drew together, and he chose his words carefully. "Why is it important to change her mind?"

"Because Jaina and Lowbacca and I are all going," Jacen said, "and . . . and it just won't be the same without her," he finished lamely.

Luke's face relaxed, and his eyes sparkled with humor. "It's not so easy to change the mind of a Force-wielding warrior from Dathomir, you know," he said.

"But it doesn't make sense that she wants to stay behind," Jacen exclaimed. "She made up some dumb excuse that it would be boring—said she was sure Corusca gems weren't any more beautiful than rainbow gems from Gallinore, and she's seen plenty of those. But she didn't *sound* bored; she sounded worried or nervous."

"We must think for ourselves," Luke said, "and sometimes that means we have to make difficult or unpopular decisions." Luke put an arm around Jacen's shoulders and led him toward the door. "Go feed your pets now. Have a safe journey to GemDiver Station—and rest assured, Tenel Ka has good reasons."

Tenel Ka woke with a start, shivering and drenched with perspiration in the cool, stone-walled chamber. Sunset-copper hair hung across her vision in tangles that had once been orderly braids. Her bedsheets were twisted about her legs as if she had been running in her sleep.

Then she remembered the dream. She *had* been running. Running from black-cloaked shadowy figures with purple-splotched faces. Muddled memories of stories her mother had told her as a child swirled through her sleep-fogged brain. She had never seen those terrifying forms before, but she knew what they were—witches from Dathomir who had drawn on the dark side of the Force to work all manner of evil.

The Nightsisters.

But the last of the Nightsisters had been destroyed or disbanded long before Tenel Ka had even been born. Why should she dream of them now? The only Force-wielders left on Dathomir used the powers of the light side.

Why these nightmares? Why now?

She squeezed her eyes shut and flopped back on her bed with a grunt as she realized what day it was. This was the day that her grandmother, Matriarch of the Hapan Royal Household, was sending an ambassador to visit Tenel Ka, heir to the Royal Throne of Hapes. And she didn't want her friends to know she was a princess. . . .

Ambassador Yfra. Tenel Ka shuddered as she thought of her iron-willed grandmother and her ambassadors, women who would lie or even kill to preserve their power—although her grandmother no longer ruled Hapes. Tenel Ka shook her head in wry amusement. The impending visit must be why she had dreamt of the Nightsisters.

Although the inhabitants of her mother's primitive planet of Dathomir and her father's plush homeworld of Hapes were light-years apart, the parallels between the Hapan politicians and the Nightsisters of Dathomir were obvious: All were power-hungry women who would stop at nothing to keep the power they craved.

Tenel Ka levered herself into a sitting position. She did not relish the idea of meeting with Ambassador Yfra. In fact, the only positive thought she could muster about it was that her friends would not be here to observe it. At least Jacen, Jaina, and Lowbacca would be far away on Lando Calrissian's GemDiver Station before the ambassador ever arrived. They would not be here to wonder why their friend, who claimed to be a simple warrior from Dathomir, was being visited by a royal ambassador from the House of Hapes. And Tenel Ka was not ready yet to explain that to them.

Well, she couldn't stay in bed any longer. She would have to get up and face whatever the day had to offer her. The meeting was unavoidable. "This," she muttered, flinging aside the covers and standing, "is a fact."

Jaina and Lowbacca sat in the center of Jaina's student quarters surrounded by a holographic map of the Yavin system.

"That ought to do it," she said. Her straight shoulder-length hair swung forward like a curtain, partially veiling her face, as she hunched over to scrutinize the input pad for her holo-projector. She had built the projector herself, piecing it together from her private stock of used electronic modules, components, cables, and other odds and ends that she kept neatly organized in a bank of bins and drawers that filled one wall of her quarters.

"Pretty impressive, huh, Lowie?" Jaina asked, flashing a lopsided grin at the ginger-furred young Wookiee. She pointed at the luminescent sphere drifting above their heads that represented the gas-giant planet of Yavin.

Lowbacca pointed to the image of a small green moon that hovered just above his left shoulder, in orbit around the big orange planet. He gave an interrogative growl.

"Ahem," the miniature translator droid Em Teedee said from the clip on Lowie's belt, as if clearing its throat. Em Teedee was roughly oval in shape, rounded in the front and flat on the back, with irregularly spaced optical sensors and a wide speaker grill at the center. "Master Lowbacca wishes to know," the miniature droid went on, "if the sphere he indicated represents the moon Yavin 4, where we are now."

"Right," said Jaina. "The gas planet Yavin has more than a dozen moons, but I haven't managed to program them all in yet. What I mainly wanted to see," she continued, "was the trajectory we're going to follow when Lando takes us to his gem-mining station in the upper atmosphere of Yavin."

Lowie growled a comment, and Jaina waited impatiently while the prissy translator droid interpreted for her.

"Of course it's a *bit* dangerous," she responded, rolling her brown eyes in exasperation, "but not much. And this is too good an opportunity to pass up. Lando's going to let us help with some of the mining operations, not just watch," Jaina said, pointing to a spot just above the glowing surface of Yavin.

Lowbacca reached for the holoprojector's input pad and pressed a few buttons. In a moment a tiny metallic-looking object appeared near the surface: GemDiver Station.

"Show-off," Jaina said, chuckling at the speed with which Lowie had programmed the holo map. "Tell you what, from now on I build 'em, you program 'em—fair enough?"

Lowie pretended to preen, rumbling his agreement as he smoothed his hand along the black streak that ran through his fur from his forehead down his back.

Just then Jacen bounded through the door. "They're here," he said breathlessly. "I mean *almost* here. They're on approach. I was in the control room and I heard that the *Lady Luck* was coming in." Twin pairs of eyes—each the color of

Corellian brandy—met in a mixture of excitement and anticipation.

"Well, then," Jaina said, "what are we waiting for?"

Jaina watched with admiration as Lando Calrissian strode down the ramp of the *Lady Luck*, an emerald-green cape billowing out behind him and a broad smile on his dark, handsome face. His frequent companion, the bald cyborg assistant Lobot, followed him down the gangplank and stood stiffly at his side.

Lando greeted Jaina with a gallant kiss on the hand before turning with a formal bow to her twin brother Jacen and Lowie. Next, he clapped the shoulder of Luke Skywalker, who had come to meet the *Lady Luck*, his barrel-shaped droid Artoo-Detoo following close behind him.

"Take good care of them, Lando," Luke said. "No unnecessary risks, okay?" Artoo added a few beeps and whistles of his own.

Lando looked at Luke, pretending to take offense. "Hey, you know I wouldn't let these kids do anything I didn't think was a safe bet."

Luke grinned and gave Lando's shoulder an affectionate slap. "That's what I'm afraid of."

"You're just worried that once they see my GemDiver Station they'll be so impressed they won't want to come back to your Jedi academy," Lando joked.

Then, with a flourish of his cape, Lando Calrissian motioned Lowie and Jacen up the ramp. He turned to Jaina. "And what can I do to make this field trip more interesting and rewarding for you, young lady?" he asked, offering her his arm to escort her into the ship.

"The first thing you can do," she said, accepting his arm with an enthusiastic smile, "is tell me all about the *Lady Luck's* engines. . . ."

2

THE *LADY LUCK* left the jewel-green jungle moon behind as Lando Calrissian and his trusted companion Lobot piloted them across space toward the gaseous ball of Yavin.

"You kids should enjoy this," Lando said. "I don't think you've seen anything quite like Corusca mining before."

As the *Lady Luck* approached the giant planet, the orbiting industrial station came into view. Lando's Corusca-mining facility, GemDiver Station, was a symphony of running lights and transmitting grids surrounded by dozens of automated defensive satellites. The security satellites homed in on the *Lady Luck*, powering up weapons as the ship approached. But when Lando keyed in an access authorization code, the satellites acknowledged his signal, then turned back to their robotic perimeter search for intruders and pirates.

"Can't have too much security," he said, "not when you're dealing with something as valuable as these Corusca gems."

Lobot, the bald, computer-enhanced human, continued his cool surveillance of the controls. Lights on the mechanical apparatus implanted on the back of Lobot's skull flashed and blinked as he studied the guidance grid and compass. Piloting smoothly, Lobot brought the *Lady Luck* into the main docking bay on GemDiver Station.

"I'm glad Luke let you come up here," Lando said, glancing back at Jacen, Jaina, and Lowie. "You can't learn everything about the universe just by sitting in the jungle and lifting rocks off the ground with your mind." He flashed a grin. "You need to broaden your horizons—learn about the way commerce works in the New Republic. That'll give you some useful knowledge, in case your lightsabers ever fail."

"We don't have lightsabers yet," Jacen said dejectedly.

"Then you might as well learn something useful in the meantime," Lando answered. Seeing Jacen's frustration, he added, "You know, your uncle Luke is concerned about your safety. He can be pretty cautious, but I trust his judgment. Don't worry, you'll get that lightsaber eventually. I bet if you just relax and stop thinking about it, you'll be practicing with a lightsaber before you know it." That said, he helped Lobot finish the landing check as the *Lady Luck* settled down in the empty bay.

Stepping out of the ship, Lando beamed and showed off his station, making enthusiastic gestures. With Lobot trailing silently behind, Lando led the three young Jedi Knights to a transparisteel viewing window that looked out at the tempestuous orangish soup of the gas giant.

Jacen pressed close to the broad window, peering down at the knotted storm systems that chained through the clouds. From this distance Yavin looked deceptively gentle in pastel yellows and whites and oranges. But he knew that even in the upper atmosphere, the winds had crushing strength, and the pressure farther down was enough to squash a ship down to a fistful of atoms.

Beside him, Jaina studied the weather patterns analytically. Lowie stood between the twins, his lanky form towering over them. He growled with amazement.

"I think it's most impressive," Em Teedee said from the clip on Lowie's belt. "And Master Lowbacca thinks so too."

GemDiver Station orbited just at the fringe of Yavin's outer atmosphere. The station's inclined orbit took it high above the planet and then dipped down to graze the gaseous levels so that Lando's Corusca gem miners could delve into the planet's deep, swirling currents.

Lando tapped his fingertip against the transparisteel window. "Far down where the atmosphere ends, the metallic core scrapes against the liquefied air. Pressures are great enough to crush elements together into extremely rare quantum crystals called Corusca gems."

Jacen perked up. "Can we see one?"

Lando thought for a moment, then nodded. "Sure. We've got a shipment ready to go out," he said. "Follow me."

With his emerald cape flowing behind him, Lando strode down the scrubbed-clean corridors. Jacen stared at the metal bulkheads, the chambers, the computer-lined offices.

The walls were smooth plasteel plates painted in soft colors and embroidered with glowing optical tubes in a variety of designs. In the background Jacen heard the faint whispering noises of forests, oceans, rivers. The soothing colors and gentle sounds made GemDiver Station an attractive place, comfortable and pleasant—not at all what he had expected.

As they approached a set of large armored doors, Lando tapped buttons in his wristlink and turned to Lobot. "Request access to security level."

Lobot mumbled something into a microphone at his collar. The sealed metal doors hissed, then slid aside to reveal an airlock chamber, the far side of which was an insulated portal providing access to open space. Four armored, conical projectiles lay on a rack; each module was only about a meter long and bristled with self-targeting lasers.

"These are the automated cargo pods," Lando said. "Because Corusca gems are so valuable, we have to take extra security precautions."

Several multiarmed droids worked busily beside the first cargo pod, an open module padded

with thick insulation. The droids' copper exoskel-
etons gleamed, as if newly polished.

"They're packing up our next shipment. Let's
take a look," Lando said.

The companions peered into the small opening
of the cargo pod, where a nimble-fingered copper
droid had packed four Corusca gems, each no
larger than Jacen's thumbnail. Lando reached in
and plucked out one of the gems.

The droid flailed its multiple hands in the air.
"Excuse me, excuse me!" it said. "Please do not
touch the gems. Excuse me!"

"It's all right," Lando said. "It's me, Lando
Calrissian."

The copper droid's flailing ceased abruptly. "Oh!
Apologies, sir," it said.

Lando shook his head. "I've got to get those
optical sensors replaced."

He held the Corusca gem between thumb and
forefinger; it glinted like liquid fire in his grasp. It
did more than just reflect light from the glowpanels on the ceiling—the Corusca gem seemed
to contain its own miniature furnace, its trapped
light bouncing around inside the crystalline facets
for ages until by sheer probability some of the
photons found their way out.

"Corusca gems have been found in no other
place in the galaxy," Lando said, "only the core
of Yavin. Of course, prospectors keep searching
other gas-giant planets, but for now my mining
station is where all Corusca gems come from. A

long time ago the Empire had a sanctioned station here. It went bankrupt pretty quickly without Imperial price supports, though. Corusca mining is a hazardous job, you know, with a high investment right from the start—but it's really paying off for me."

He let Jacen, Jaina, and Lowie hold the gem and marvel at its beauty "Corusca gems are the hardest substance known," he said. "They can slice through transparisteel like a laser goes through Sullustan jam."

The nervous packing droid plucked the gem from Lowbacca's hairy hand and replaced it in the cargo pod, packing extra sealant around the stones before it closed the access port. The droid engaged a sequence of controls on the back of the cargo pod, and the bristling spines of self-targeting lasers raised themselves up to their armed position.

"Cargo pod ready for launch," the copper droid said. "Please leave the launching bay."

Lando ushered the three kids out of the room, and the heavy metal doors sealed behind him as the droids scurried about their tasks. "Over here. We can watch through the outer port," he said. "This cargo pod is a hyperspace projectile targeted to my broker on Borgo Prime, who distributes the Corusca gems for a percentage of the profits."

They pressed together at a thick round window that looked away from the planet out into space.

As they watched, the cargo pod shot out of the launching bay, then hovered to reorient itself and adjust its coordinates. The bright light of its thrusters traced a line across the blackness of space.

Satellites around GemDiver Station rotated as their sensors tracked the pod, aiming their own weapons; but the cargo pod apparently sent the proper ID signals, and the defensive satellites left it alone. Then, in a blur of motion, the pod streaked forward, flashing into hyperspace with a wealth of Corusca gems in its belly.

"Hey, Lando, can we help you do some of the gem mining?" Jacen asked.

"Yes, we'd like to see how it's done," Jaina added.

"I don't know . . . ," Lando said. "It's tough work, and a little risky."

"So is training to be a Jedi Knight," Jaina pointed out, "as we've already seen. Don't you think learning is worth a bit of risk?"

Lowbacca growled a comment.

"What do you mean you're willing to take the risk?" Em Teedee said. "Dear me, I believe Master Calrissian was actually emphasizing the hazards in the hope that you would *not* want to go."

"Well, we'd like to go anyway," Jacen piped up.

Lando held up a hand, grinning as if he had just thought of something—though Jacen could sense that he had been planning it all along. "Well, maybe it *is* time I got back to doing some real work around here instead of all this management stuff. All right, I'll take you down myself."

To Jacen, the Submersible Mining Environment looked like a large diving bell. Its hull was thickly armored, a dull gray with oily smears of color that reflected weirdly in the lights. The hatch appeared thick and durable enough to withstand turbolaser fire.

"This is called the *Fast Hand*," Lando said, "a little ship we designed exclusively for going to the greatest depths of Yavin 4. It's gone almost all the way to the core, where we can reach the biggest Corusca stones." He ran his fingers over the oily hull plating.

"The *Fast Hand* is covered with a fine skin of quantum armor," Lando said, awe apparent in his voice, "a little something developed by the Empire. But we turned the military applications to our own uses—the ultimate in commercial spin-off technology." Lando sounded as if he were giving a speech to a board of directors, and then he remembered his audience. "Well, never mind. The armor on this baby is strong enough to withstand even the pressures deep in Yavin's core. We'll be lowered down, connected to GemDiver Station by an energy tether—like an unbreakable magnetic rope."

"Not even the storms can snap it?" Jaina asked.

Lando spread his hands wide, dismissing her concern. "We might get jostled around a bit, but . . ." He laughed. "The seats are padded. We'll be okay."

Lowbacca stooped, but still banged his head on the low doorway as he climbed into the diving bell. Jacen and Jaina jumped in after him. As Lando followed them into the *Fast Hand*, he pulled the hatch shut.

He rapped his knuckles against the inside wall with a metallic thump. "Safe and sound," he said, then settled into the cushioned seat in front of the piloting controls. Jacen strapped into the copilot's chair beside him, while Jaina and Lowie took the rear seats. Thick, square windows covered the walls and floor, giving them a view no matter which way they looked.

"Oh my, isn't this exciting?" Em Teedee said. Lowie grunted in agreement.

3

LANDO KEYED IN some instructions on the control panel. "I'm telling Lobot we're ready for departure."

Red lights flashed on the bay walls, signaling the *Fast Hand*'s status as it prepared for release into Yavin's atmosphere. Three technicians trotted out of the room, and the airlock doors sealed behind them.

"Hang on," Lando said.

The floor beneath the *Fast Hand* slid away. Jacen's stomach lurched as the armored diving bell fell from GemDiver Station, down into the swirling fury of gases. Lowie yelped in sudden astonishment. Jacen's pulse raced. Jaina gripped the arms of her seat.

The *Fast Hand* hurtled downward, but soon Jacen sensed their descent stabilizing, slowing, becoming more controlled.

"I can feel the energy tether holding us," Jaina said.

Jacen reached out with his Jedi senses and

detected a shimmering cool thread that connected them to the orbiting station high above. Eager and interested, he unclasped his crash restraints and looked out the nearest windowport as the roiling clouds rushed closer, slamming toward them.

Jacen saw a fleet of tiny ships like agricultural drones skimming across the tops of the rising gases. The small ships hauled a glowing golden web behind them, like a faint net dragged through the clouds.

"What are those?" Jaina asked, curious as always about how things worked.

"Contractors of mine," Lando said. "Corusca fishermen. They take a fleet of skiffs along the cloud tops, trailing an energy seine behind them. As they fly through the clouds, the energy differential in the net reacts to the presence of tiny Corusca stones. They pick up only smaller stones and Corusca dust. It may not seem like much, but it's still quite valuable and worth the effort.

"I help support their operation, and they give me a percentage of their catch. But the larger Corusca gems are deeper down. The great pressures near the core always made it impossible to mine those big gemstones, but with this new quantum armor, we can take the *Fast Hand* all the way down."

"Well, what are we waiting for?" Jaina asked.

"Right. Let's go," Jacen said, rubbing his hands together. Then he flashed a mischievous grin. "Hey, Lando, I heard two droids talking the other day. The first one said, 'Well, did you beat the Wookiee at sabacc?' and the second one said—"

"—'Yes, but it cost me an arm and a leg,'" Lando finished. "That's an old joke, kid."

Jacen frowned at first, then giggled. "Maybe that's why Tenel Ka didn't laugh at it."

Jaina looked at her brother. "I don't think that's the reason she didn't laugh."

The diving bell continued its descent. Lando plied the controls, unreeling the energy tether. As the dense organic mists and colored aerosols folded around them, the winds became gentle fingers drumming against the walls, growing louder and more insistent.

The storm systems increased in fury. Bolts of blue lightning shot across the murky sky as far as Jacen could see. Static electricity crawled over the outer hull like jagged caterpillars, sparking and snapping against the connecting point of the energy tether.

Lowie uttered a long and concerned-sounding sentence in Wookiee language, and his translator droid piped up. "A good question, Master Lowbacca. What *does* happen if the energy tether is severed? How would we get back?"

"Oh, we've got life-support supplies aboard," Lando said, waving his hand again. "We could survive quite a while down here until a rescue mission was mounted from GemDiver Station. We have communications and energy backups— but it won't happen, don't worry."

As if to disagree with him, an unexpected gust

of wind slapped them sideways so that Jacen tumbled from his seat. He pulled himself back up and sheepishly refastened his crash webbing.

Suddenly the *Fast Hand* seemed to snap free from its connecting line. They dropped like a cannonball, plunging and plunging for a full ten seconds. Lowie yowled, and Jacen and Jaina cried out. Lando pumped up the energy levels until finally he managed to reconnect the tether.

"See? No problem," he said with a nonchalant grin, but Jacen could see the beads of sweat on Lando's forehead. "You all might want to tighten your crash webbing, though," he said. "These storms make for some hefty turbulence in the lower atmosphere. That's what stirs up the interface level and gives the Corusca gems a nudge. Once we get a little lower, we'll start hunting."

"I'd like to try my hand at it," Jaina said.

"I'll let you each have a turn at the controls, but I should warn you that Corusca gems are very rare, even down here. Don't expect to find anything."

Jacen asked, "If we're at the controls and we find a Corusca gem, can we keep it?"

Lando smiled indulgently. "Well, I suppose . . . but we can't spend a lot of time down here looking for gems."

"Oh, we won't," Jacen said. "But it's still good to have some incentive."

Lando laughed. "Just like your father," he said. Jacen smiled, thinking of all the times Lando Calrissian and Han Solo had worked with each

other—or in competition against each other—
over the years of their long friendship.

Lando looked at his controls again and opened
up more window panels on the floor so they could
see the murky gases beneath them, supercharged
with energy.

"This is probably good enough," Lando said.
"Let's start fishing." He glanced at the chronometer on his wrist. "We really need to head back up
soon." He swallowed, and Jacen sensed just how
nervous Lando really was to be down this far.
Daredevil gem hunters willing to risk their lives
for the fabulously expensive Corusca stones usually did all the deep dives.

The *Fast Hand* had gone so far into the plan-
etary atmosphere that by now the winds were
dark around them, so dense that even light from
Yavin's sun could not penetrate. Lando clicked on
the diving bell's spotlights, and cones of creamy
light struggled against the battering storms and
whirling gases.

"I'm going to deploy our trolling cables," Lando
said. "They're electromagnetic ropes that dangle
down to catch flying Corusca gems whipped up by
the storms. You can each have only a few minutes,
because we need to get back up to the station.
These storm systems are getting worse."

The storms hadn't seemed to be getting worse at
all to Jacen; they had been bad enough to begin
with. But the tension apparent on Lando's face

made Jacen want to end their expedition quickly as well.

"Lowbacca, why don't you try first?" Lando suggested. "Come up front and take the controls."

The young Wookiee crouched in a seat that was far too small for him and rested his hands on the multiple joysticks of the controls. He directed the dangling, sizzling energy cables that trailed out like magnetic tentacles through the stormy atmosphere.

Jacen unbuckled his crash webbing again and crawled along the floor to peer through the square portholes. He could see the yellow magnetic whips that extended from the *Fast Hand* raking through the gaseous clouds, but catching nothing.

After a few moments, Lowie groaned in frustration. Em Teedee said, "Master Lowbacca wishes to offer someone else a turn." Lowie relinquished the controls to Jaina, who sat down with focused concentration, the tip of her tongue wedged between her lips at the corner of her mouth. Her eyes, golden-brown pools that stared into nothingness, fell half-closed as she worked the controls. Jacen watched the energy lines writhe below, sifting through the clouds, searching.

"Now, don't get disappointed," Lando said. "I told you it's still hard work to find even one gem. They're quite rare. If they weren't, they wouldn't be so valuable."

Jaina continued to search for a few minutes longer, then gave up. Jacen climbed to his feet and came forward, struggling to keep his balance in the gale-force winds. He caught the arm of the chair and pulled himself into it, letting his hands wrap around the controls.

As he tugged on the joysticks he could feel the response from the lashing energy cables, groping about like nimble fingers sifting through sand to find gold. He reached out with his mind, concentrating as Jaina had, using what he knew of Jedi powers to search for the precious gems. He didn't know what a Corusca stone would *feel* like, but he expected he would know if he encountered one. The whirling clouds seemed empty, thick with useless gases and crushed debris, nothing of interest.

His twin sister sat behind him, and he could feel her hoping for his success. Just as he was about to give up, Jacen suddenly felt a flash, a glint in his mind. He nudged the joysticks sideways, stretching out the long electrical fingers, searching, extending them as far as they would reach. With one lightning tip he scratched through the clouds, stretching, *stretching* . . . and finally he snagged the glimmer in his mind.

The control panels lit up. "I got one!" he cried.

Lando looked as shocked as anyone else. "You did!" he said. "Okay, let's bring it in fast. Time to go."

Lando took over and reeled the magnetic tentacles back into the *Fast Hand*, pulling in the catch. As he stabilized the energy tether again, Lando opened a small access port in the floor and pulled up a durasteel cargo box rimed with frost. He withdrew an irregular but beautiful Corusca gem, larger than the one he had shown them earlier. It flashed with trapped fire.

Breathlessly, Jacen took it from Lando, cradling it in the palms of his hands. "Look what I got!" he said.

Jaina and Lowie offered their congratulations. Lando, knowing he had promised to give the prize to the kids, shook his head in grudging admiration. "Keep that safe, Jacen," Lando said. "That's enough to buy half a city block on Coruscant, I bet."

"It's worth *that* much?" Jacen ran his fingers along the smooth, incredibly hard surface of the gem. "What if I lose it?" he said.

"Put it in your boot," Jaina said. "You know you never lose things there."

"I will," Jacen agreed. "I think I'll give it to mother for her next birthday."

Lando slapped his forehead. "Even Han never gave Leia something that valuable! Almost makes me wish I had a couple of kids," he muttered. "All right, let's head back up."

As if to encourage him, another fist of wind slammed the side of the *Fast Hand* and sent them spinning. Jacen fumbled with his Corusca gem, nearly dropped it on the floor, then caught it again and clutched it in his fist. He immediately tucked it into his boot, where he wouldn't have to worry about it falling out.

His forehead still furrowed with anxiety, Lando Calrissian reeled in the energy tether, hauling the

Fast Hand back toward the safer levels of Yavin's atmosphere.

The storms tossed them around. Once they heard a loud *spang* against the quantum-armored hull. Lando yelped and looked over at the wall. "Another one! Jaina, get over there and check that seal," he said.

"What happened?" Jacen asked.

On her knees, Jaina scuttled over to check. "Looks like it's okay," she said.

"What was it?" Jacen insisted. He saw the tiniest dent on the inside, but sensed no leaking atmosphere.

"We just got hit by a Corusca gem thrown at high speed by these winds. It's like a projectile weapon striking us, and only the quantum armor saved us. I can't believe this luck." Lando shook his head. "I spend hours and hours looking for those gems on my own and come up empty-handed. But when I bring you down here, Jacen snatches one right away, and then we get hit by another as we're heading back up top."

Lowie bellowed a comment, and Em Teedee said, "I fervently agree with Master Lowbacca: Let's hope we don't encounter any more of them."

Lightning bolts flashed around the hull, sparking blue light into the murky clouds. But as they rose higher toward the safety of GemDiver Station, the storm winds grew calmer, less insistent. Lando relaxed visibly.

When they finally rose back into the glittering

GemDiver Station, and the floor sealed beneath them, Lando heaved a sigh of relief and slumped down in the pilot's chair.

The pressure bay refilled with atmosphere, and Lando flicked the controls to unseal the armored hatch. "There. We're back safe and sound," he said, climbing out on unsteady legs. "I think that's enough adventures for now. How about we relax and get something to eat?"

Lando had barely finished making the suggestion, though, when the sudden wailing of station alarms screeched across the intercom systems.

"Now what is it?" Lando asked. "What's going on?"

The three young Jedi Knights jumped out of the *Fast Hand* and followed Lando as he ran to a comm station on the wall. "This is Lando Calrissian. Give me a status update."

"An unidentified fleet just appeared out of hyperspace," came the tense voice of a station security chief. "They refuse our hails and are heading toward GemDiver Station at great speed, intent unknown." The voice clicked off.

Jacen and Jaina ran toward one of the viewports and looked out into the darkness of space. Then Jacen saw the ships, like a swarm of meteors, streaking in their direction. Somehow he sensed they were powering on their weapons—up to no good. He gulped.

"Looks like an Imperial fleet to me," Jaina said.

4

LANDO RUSHED TOWARD the control bridge of GemDiver Station. "Come on, kids. Follow me!" he shouted.

Jaina took the lead while Lowie and Jacen followed at a run. Lowie's long Wookiee legs nearly made him plow over Lando in his haste. "Oh, *do* be careful, Lowbacca!" Em Teedee called.

Taking a turbolift to the upper observation tower, they bustled onto the control bridge, a cylindrical turret that protruded above the main armored body of GemDiver Station. Narrow rectangular windows encircled the control room, allowing a full view in all directions. The glowing diagnostic screens directly below each viewport flashed alarm warnings. Lando's armed guards ran about, strapping additional weapons to their belts, preparing to defend the station.

"We are under attack, sir," Lobot murmured in his quiet, difficult-to-hear voice. The cyborg was a blur of motion, hands darting from keyboard to keyboard, eyes scanning the screens around him and silently assessing details. The lights on the computer implants at the sides of his head flashed like fireworks.

Lando scanned the narrow observation ports and saw the fleet of ships coming in from deep space. "Do you think they're pirates?" he asked. Then to the twins and Lowie, he said reassuringly, "Don't worry. We're got station security on alert. These people don't have a chance against our defenses."

Jaina studied one of the diagnostic screens, pursing her lips. She shook her head. "Not just pirates," she said, recognizing some of the ships by the ellipsoid shape of their main body, engine turrets swept back like jagged wings on top and bottom. "Imperial craft. The four on the outside are Skipray blastboats, each fully equipped with three ion cannons, proton torpedo launcher, concussion missiles, and two fire-linked laser cannons."

Lando seemed startled. "Yeah, that's right."

She looked calmly up at his surprised expression. "Dad had me study a lot of ships. Believe me, these're more than even your security systems could hope to fight."

Lando clapped a hand to his forehead and groaned. "That's not just a pirate fleet, that's an armada! What's the big ship in the middle? I don't recognize it."

In her mind Jaina ran through mechanical specifications of all the ship designs she had learned from her father—but right now she was at a loss.

"Some kind of modified assault shuttle, maybe?" Jaina said. Through the magnification on the screens they stared as the ships came relentlessly in. "But I don't understand that contraption in the bow."

The mysterious assault shuttle had a strange device mounted at its front end, circular and jagged, like the wide-open mouth of a fanged underwater predator.

"Send a distress signal," Lando said to Lobot. "Full spectrum. Make sure *everybody* knows we're under attack here."

With maddening computer-enhanced calm, Lobot shook his bald head. "I've already tried. We're jammed, sir—can't punch a signal through their screens."

"Well, what do they want?" Lando asked in exasperation.

"They've made no demands," Lobot replied. "They refuse to answer our hails. We do not know what they're after."

Jaina stared out the window at the incoming ships and felt cold inside. She shuddered. Jacen squeezed her hand, his forehead wrinkled with anxiety. They had realized the same thing.

"I've got a bad feeling about this," Jacen said. "It's . . . *us* they want, isn't it?"

"Yeah, I can feel it," Jaina said, her voice barely above a whisper. Lowie nodded his shaggy head and groaned in agreement.

"What do you kids mean?" Lando looked at

them with disbelief in his large brown eyes. "They *must* be after our Corusca gems—it's the only thing that makes sense."

Jaina shook her head, but Lando was too busy to pay further attention. The four flanking blast-boats angled out from the central assault shuttle toward the defensive satellites surrounding Gem-Diver Station.

"Have you removed the fail-safes from the targeting systems?" Lando asked.

Lobot nodded. "Systems ready to fire," he murmured. High-powered lasers from the defensive satellites lanced out toward the blastboats, but the small satellites could not generate enough power to penetrate the heavy Imperial armor.

Each Skipray blastboat targeted one of the small satellites and unleashed a crackling blur from its ion cannons. The defensive satellites powered up, preparing to fire again, but then all the lights went dead.

"The ion cannons fried the circuits," Lobot announced in his calm voice. "All satellites are off-line."

The Skiprays came in for another strike and fired with laser cannons, this time blasting the defensive satellites into molten metal vapor.

"We've still got the station's armor," Lando said, but now his trembling voice betrayed his lack of confidence.

The modified assault shuttle in the middle of the armada homed in on one of the lower space doors. From the bottom decks of the station came a loud *thump* and *clang* as something large and heavy struck the outer hull—and stayed.

"What are they doing?" Lando asked.

"The modified assault shuttle has attached itself to the outer wall of GemDiver Station," Lobot reported.

"Where?"

The bald cyborg checked readings. "One of the equipment bays. I think they're trying to force their way in."

Lando waved his hand in dismissal. "Well, they can knock but they can't come in." He smiled nervously. "Just keep all the airlocks sealed. Our station armor should hold."

"Excuse me," Jaina said, "but I may have figured out what that modification is. I think they plan to bore through the station walls. The jagged things we saw looked like teeth—so I'm guessing they cut through metal."

"Not *this* metal." Lando shook his head. "The station wall is double-armored. Nothing could cut through it."

Jacen spoke up. "I thought you said Corusca gems could cut through anything."

Lando shook his head again. "Sure, but that would take a whole shipment of industrial-grade Corusca gems." Then he stopped, eyes widening. "Well, uh, we *have* shipped some industrial-grade gems since we upgraded our operations."

He picked up a comlink and spoke into it. "This

is Lando Calrissian. All security details go to lower equipment bay number"—he leaned over Lobot's shoulder to look at the screen—"number thirty-four. Full armor and weapons. We're about to be boarded by hostile forces."

Lando took a blaster pistol from the sealed armory case inside the bridge deck. He turned to Lobot. "*Nobody* boards my station without my permission." He started down the corridor, calling over his shoulder as he ran. "You kids find a safe place, and stay there!"

So of course the young Jedi Knights followed him.

Station guards in padded, dark blue uniforms sprinted from corridor intersections. The pastel colors and nature sounds of GemDiver Station seemed oddly out of place, no longer soothing amid the chaos of defensive preparations and the turmoil of screeching alarms.

By the time they reached lower equipment bay 34, a squad of station guards had already set up their position behind storage containers and supply modules, blaster rifles drawn and aimed at the wall.

Jaina heard a whining, gnawing sound that made her teeth vibrate. A circular section of the outer wall glowed, and she could imagine the assault shuttle on the other side, linked to Gem-Diver Station like a huge battle-ready brine-eel, chewing its way through the station armor.

A bright white line appeared in the circle as a Corusca tooth bit through the thick plate. Jaina hoped belatedly that the attacking ship's seal against the station was airtight.

One of Lando's station guards, keyed up with overwhelming tension, let off two shots from his blaster rifle. The bolts spanged against the wall and left a discolored blotch on the inner hull, but the jaws of the boring machine continued to chew through the plates.

In a flash, with a puff of steam and the *crump* of small, shaped explosives, a large disk of the outer hull fell forward into the equipment bay.

Lando's security forces started firing immediately, even before the smoke cleared; but the enemy on the other side did not pause either. Dozens of white-armored Imperial stormtroopers boiled through the hole like a hive of frenzied lizard-ants that Jacen had once kept in his collection of exotic pets. The stormtroopers fired as they charged—using only the curving blue arcs of stun beams, Jaina was relieved to see.

Four stormtroopers went down with smoking holes in their white armor; but more and more poured out of the assault shuttle. The air in the equipment bay was crisscrossed with bright weapons fire.

Looming behind the armed stormtroopers, cloaked in shadows and rising smoke, stood a tall and sinister woman dressed in a black cape with spines on each shoulder. She had flowing ebony hair like the wings of a bird of prey. Despite her growing terror, Jaina saw that the woman's eyes were a striking color, like the violet of iridescent jungle flowers on Yavin 4. Jaina felt her heart clench as if hands of ice had wrapped around it.

The ominous dark woman stepped through the smoldering hole in the wall of GemDiver Station, oblivious to the weapons fire. A faint electric-blue corona of static lightning clung around her like the powerful discharges that had zapped the *Fast Hand* in the atmospheric storms of Yavin.

"Remember—don't harm the children," the woman shouted. Her voice was slow and heavy, but razor-sharp menace edged every word.

At the mention of the children, Lando whirled to see that the twins and Lowie had followed him. "What are you doing here?" he said. "Come on, we've got to get you to safety!" He waved his blaster pistol toward the entryway. Then, as if in afterthought, he turned and fired three more times, catching one of the white-armored storm-troopers full in the chest.

Jacen and Jaina bolted down the corridor. Lowie, needing no further encouragement, bellowed as he ran along.

Lando came charging after. "I guess you were right," he said, panting. "For some reason they *are* after you."

"I'm just a simple droid," Em Teedee wailed. "I certainly hope they don't want me."

A series of muffled explosions erupted behind them, and a shockwave of heat rippled through the station's metal corridors, making the kids stumble.

Lando caught his balance and steadied Jaina. "Turn right," he gasped. "Up here."

They ran. More blaster fire followed them, then a third explosion. Lando clenched his teeth. "This has *not* been a good day," he grumbled.

"I most heartily concur," Em Teedee chimed from Lowie's waist.

"Here! In the shipping chamber." Lando gestured for the three others to stop outside the barricaded door of the launching room where they had seen the cargo pods and the droids packing Corusca gems for automated shipment.

He punched in an access code, but Lando's fingers were trembling. A red light blinked. "ACCESS DENIED." Lando hissed something, then rekeyed the number. This time the light winked green, and the heavy triple doors sighed open. Inside, the two copper-plated droids continued packing the hyperpods. "Excuse me," one droid said, sounding flustered, "would you please discontinue those explosions? The vibrations make it much more difficult for us to process."

Lando ignored the droids as he pushed the kids inside. "We can't get you away from here—those blastboats would come after you before you knew it—but this is the safest place on the station. I'll stand outside and guard the door." He gripped his blaster pistol, feigning confidence.

Lowie growled, obviously wanting to fight; but before Jacen or Jaina could say anything, Lando slapped the emergency panel. The thick doors clanged shut, locking them inside the chamber.

Jacen placed his ear against the thick door and listened, but he could hear only the muffled noises of battle. Lowie, his ginger-colored fur standing on end with battle-readiness, kneaded his big knuckles. Jaina looked around the room for anything to help them fight.

Jacen yelled to the droids, "Hey, is there an armory in here? Do you have any weapons?"

The droids interrupted their packing and swiveled smooth copper heads toward him, optical sensors glowing. "Please do not disturb us, sir," they said, then resumed their tasks. "We have essential work to do."

Outside the door, the sound of gunfire suddenly increased. Jaina pulled Jacen back from the door as she heard Lando shout. The door vibrated with the impact of energy bolts, then everything went quiet. Jaina waited, backing away and looking into her twin brother's brandy-brown eyes. They both swallowed. Lowbacca let out a thin sound like a whimper. The multiarmed droids continued working, undisturbed.

A shower of sparks ran around part of the door as heavy-duty lasers cut into it, slicing away a section.

"D'you suppose you could invent some sort of weapon for us in the next few seconds?" Jacen said.

Jaina racked her brain for inspiration, but her inventiveness failed her.

The door split open, melted and smoking. The security breach set off yet another alarm, but the sounds were pitiful and superfluous in the already-overwhelming noise of the battle for GemDiver Station.

Stormtroopers muscled their way in.

The two packing droids trundled indignantly toward the stormtroopers. "Intruder alert," one of the droids said. "Warning. No unauthorized entry is permitted. You must return to—"

In response, the stormtroopers fired with all their weapons, blasting both copper droids into shards of smoking components that clattered and sparked on the floor.

Jaina saw Lando sprawled unconscious on the floor outside the door, his green cape pooled around him, his right arm extended forward, still grasping the blaster pistol.

The towering dark woman strode in, her violet eyes flashing at the three companions. The stormtroopers leveled blaster pistols at Jacen, Jaina, and Lowbacca.

"Wait!" Jaina said. "What do you want?"

"Do not let them manipulate your minds," the dark woman shouted to the stormtroopers. "Stun them!"

Before Jaina could say anything else, bright blue arcs shot toward her and the others, and they were overcome by a wave of unconsciousness.

Jaina fell into blackness.

5

ON YAVIN 4 TENEL Ka paced the ramparts of the Great Temple that housed Luke Skywalker's Jedi academy. As befitted a warrior of Dathomir, she wore scaled armor that shone as if it had just been polished . . . which it had. Her red-gold hair was caught up in a multitude of ceremonial braids, each decorated with feathers or beads. Her cool gray eyes scanned the leaden skies for any sign of the ship that would bring the dreaded ambassador from her grandmother.

Wind whipped the ornamented braids about her face, and Tenel Ka pushed them away in annoyance. The humid air felt oppressive, charged with menace. Yavin's dry season had ended.

She sensed an uncomfortable tingling in the depths of her mind that told her something was about to happen, as if lightning were about to strike. She sighed. Her grandmother's messengers and diplomats could be as lethal as lightning. . . .

They were not above killing an enemy, or even a friend, to ensure that the successor to the throne of Hapes was the one they most desired to have in power. It was rumored that her grandmother's assassins had murdered Tenel Ka's own uncle, brother to her father, Prince Isolder.

She started in surprise as a raindrop, warm as blood, landed with a splat on her bare arm. Although the air was not cold, she shivered.

Her feelings toward her grandmother were complex: she both admired and despised the older woman. Tenel Ka preferred to dress in the lizard-skin armor of the warrior women of Dathomir, like her mother, rather than in the fine web-silks of the Royal House of the Hapes Cluster.

So far, Tenel Ka had managed to tread a fine line between pleasing and annoying her grandmother. She knew that if she stepped over that line too far, assassins might someday pay her a visit. . . .

A branch of lightning crackled across the ominous sky, followed by a boom of thunder. Atop the temple, Tenel Ka paced like a caged animal, her agitation increasing as she stalked along the edge of the pyramid and wondered why Ambassador Yfra did not come. So great was her turmoil that she didn't even notice that Luke Skywalker had joined her on the observation deck until he stood directly in front of her.

The Jedi Master placed both of his hands on her shoulders and looked into her eyes. Peace and warmth flowed from him, and Tenel Ka felt herself begin to relax. "There's a message in the

Comm Center for you," he said quietly. "Would you like me to be present while you speak with the ambassador?"

Tenel Ka could not suppress a shudder of revulsion as she thought of her grandmother's thin-lipped emissary. "Your presence would"—she paused for a moment, searching for words—"honor me, Master Skywalker."

Tenel Ka stood erect, holding her head high as she faced her grandmother's ambassador in the Comm Center viewscreen—an image that for all its apparent cruelty still held traces of proud beauty. Ambassador Yfra's hair and eyes were the color of polished pewter.

"Our meetings on Coruscant took longer than we anticipated, young one," Yfra was saying in a voice that indicated she was not used to being questioned. "Therefore, our meeting with you must be postponed for two days."

Tenel Ka gave no outward sign of her discomposure, but her heart sank. Jacen, Jaina, and Lowbacca were due back long before then. She sent a pleading glance to Luke.

The Jedi Master stepped forward and spoke in a soft voice. "Perhaps I could bring the Princess of Hapes to meet with you on Coruscant?" he offered.

Ambassador Yfra smiled in what Tenel Ka knew was meant to be a kindly fashion, but there was no kindness or conciliation in her eyes. "I have specific orders to observe the heir of Hapes in her place of study."

Tenel Ka opened her mouth to speak, but was spared the necessity when an emergency beacon flashed next to the screen. Luke reacted instantly. "Ambassador Yfra, we have a priority override communication coming in. Please wait," he said, switching the channel before the ambassador had a chance to reply.

The dark face of Lando Calrissian appeared, his handsome features marred by a worried frown. Confusion haunted his bleary eyes. His hair and clothes were disheveled, and warning sirens whooped in the background.

"Luke, buddy," he rasped, "I'm not sure exactly what happened. They . . . fried our security satellites, boarded the station . . . must've stunned us. We're okay, but—" Lando's troubled eyes closed and his jaw tightened, "Jacen, Jaina, and Lowbacca are gone. They've been kidnapped."

Luke drew in a deep breath. Tenel Ka guessed he was using a Jedi calming technique, but with less success than usual. His body appeared relaxed, but his clear blue eyes carried a laser-sharp look. One hand was clenched into a fist at his side. "Who did this?" he asked, his voice terse.

Lando shook his head. "We don't know who has the kids or why, but I've got all my best people working on it. It was someone connected with the Empire, though—that's for sure."

"I'll be there within the hour," Luke said, reaching for the comlink.

"Wait," Tenel Ka said. "These are my friends. I know how they think. I know what they would do. I cannot cower here while they are in danger. Please. I must go with you."

Luke nodded. "Your presence would . . . honor me," he answered, echoing her earlier words. His eyes went back to Lando's image. "*We'll* be there within the hour," he amended, then switched back to the ambassador's comm frequency.

Ambassador Yfra's mouth was open as if she were prepared to protest such rude treatment, but Luke spoke first. "I'm sorry to keep you waiting, Ambassador, but an emergency has come up. It requires both my presence and that of the princess. I'm afraid we must postpone any plans to meet with you until this situation is resolved. Please convey our respectful greetings to the Royal House of Hapes." With a slight bow, he snapped off the comm channel.

Even though she was worried about her friends, a feeling of satisfaction bubbled up within Tenel Ka at the deftness with which Master Skywalker had handled Ambassador Yfra.

Luke looked at Tenel Ka. "I'm sure the ambassador isn't used to being postponed with so little explanation, but we have more important things to do right now."

Tenel Ka nodded emphatically. "This is a fact."

• • •

Tenel Ka tried to be impartial and unemotional as Master Skywalker expertly guided the shuttle toward GemDiver Station. She needed to remain unruffled and alert, to search for any clue that might help them recover the three young Jedi— the best friends she'd ever had.

The multicolored lights of the station winked as the docking-bay doors slid open and Luke brought the shuttle in for a landing. At any other time Tenel Ka might have noted her surroundings, the artistry and craftsmanship that had gone into the station's construction—but the moment the shuttle doors opened, she was assailed by a sense of lingering violence and darkness. Of *wrongness*.

Harried and disheveled, Lando Calrissian met them at the shuttle. Motioning for Luke and Tenel Ka to follow, he led them to the sealed shipping bay where the final struggle had occurred.

Tenel Ka swept the chamber with her eyes, noting the blaster burns on the walls and ceiling of the outer corridor, the congealed rivulets of molten plasteel, the shards of broken metal. Then she watched as Luke sank down on one knee, placed both hands against the floor, and let his eyes flutter closed.

"Yes, it happened here," he murmured. He took a few deep breaths, then fixed Lando with the piercing blueness of his gaze. "Don't blame yourself," he said. "You fought well."

Lando's face was filled with regret, and he shook his head. "But it wasn't enough, buddy. I couldn't save them." A note of anger and self-reproach crept into his voice. "I was too busy trying to defend my station—thinking they were pirates come to steal my Corusca gems. I didn't even realize they were after the kids until it was too late."

Luke neither condemned nor pardoned Lando, Tenel Ka noticed. He simply listened.

At last Lando spoke again in a quiet voice. "If there's anything you need to help find them—my station, a ship, a crew . . . anything at all—"

Lando's offer of help was cut short by the arrival of his assistant Lobot, whose computer headset flashed with an ever-changing array of lights. "We finished patching the hull breach in lower equipment bay thirty-four," he said without preamble.

Lando turned to Luke and Tenel Ka, his forehead creasing into an indignant scowl. "They sliced us open like a disposable can of emergency rations."

The bald cyborg nodded in corroboration. "Their equipment was specially designed to remove a section of hull."

Lando continued, "The only thing I know of sharp enough to slice through durasteel that quickly is—"

"Corusca gems," Luke finished for him.

"Industrial grade," Lobot added.

"Right," Lando said morosely. "They used *our own gems* against us."

"Rare and expensive," Lobot said. "Not just anyone could purchase them."

Tenel Ka saw Luke's eyes light with sudden hope. "Can you tell us where your shipments of such gems were sold?"

Lando shrugged. "Like my friend said, industrial-grade gems are fairly rare. We've made only two shipments since our operation opened." He sent a questioning glance at his cyborg assistant.

Lobot pressed a panel on the back of his head and cocked it to one side as if listening to a voice no one else could hear. A moment later he nodded. "Both shipments were sold through our broker on Borgo Prime."

"Can you find out who he sold them to?" Luke asked.

"I doubt it," Lando said. "Gem brokers are pretty skittish. They pay a good percentage, but they're secretive —afraid that if we know who their customers are, we won't need the middlemen anymore."

"Then we must go to Borgo Prime and find out ourselves," Tenel Ka said with fierce determination.

Luke sent her a warm smile, then turned back to Lando. "What is Borgo Prime anyway?"

"An asteroid spaceport and trade center. It's also a hangout for merchants, thieves, murderers, smugglers . . . the dregs of the galaxy." Lando flashed Luke a grin. "A lot like Mos Eisley on Tatooine. You'll feel right at home."

Tenel Ka waited in silence as Master Skywalker faced the screen in GemDiver Station's Communications Center.

Han Solo stood with one arm around his wife, Leia, who was supported on the other side by Lowie's uncle, Chewbacca.

Tenel Ka studied the images on the screen and decided that at this moment Leia Organa Solo looked more like a concerned mother than a powerful politician.

"But Luke, they're *our* children," she was saying. "We can't simply stand by and do nothing if they're in danger."

"Not on your life!" Han said.

"Of course not," Luke agreed quietly. "But as the New Republic's chief of state, you can't afford to put yourself in that same danger. Mobilize your forces. Start an investigation. Send out spies and probe droids. But stay there and act as a central clearinghouse for information."

"All right, Luke," Leia said. "We'll work from Coruscant for now, but once we've done everything we can from here, we'll go looking for them ourselves."

"I'll come get you in the *Falcon*," Han said.

"Give me ten standard days first," Luke said. "I have a lead I'm going to follow right now before the trail gets cold. We need to get going. We'll keep you informed of our progress."

"We?" Han asked. "Is Lando going with you?"

"No," Luke replied. "The heir of Hapes will honor me with her company," he said, gesturing to Tenel Ka.

"We are grateful for your assistance," Leia said formally.

Tenel Ka nodded toward the screen with a brief, stiff bow. "Jacen, Jaina, and Lowbacca have a greater call on me than honor," she said. "They have my friendship."

Leia's face softened. "Then I owe you my gratitude as a mother as well." Chewbacca rumbled what Tenel Ka could only interpret as an agreement.

"Don't worry, we'll find them," Luke said, his voice filled with urgency. "But we need to leave now."

Han lifted his chin and smiled at Luke. "Okay, get going, kid."

Just before the communications link was broken, Leia spoke again. "And may the Force be with you."

6

JAINA CAME BACK to consciousness with Lowie shaking her shoulders. The lanky Wookiee moaned plaintively until she groaned and woke up, blinking her eyes.

A rush of unpleasant sensations flooded through her: queasy stomach, pounding head, aching joints—aftereffects of the stormtroopers' stun beams. The human body wasn't designed to be knocked out with a blast of energy. Her ears hummed, too, but her instincts told her that the sounds were real—the rumbling vibrations of a big ship in hyperdrive.

Uncertain about whether she dared risk a more vertical position, Jaina cautiously turned her head. She saw that she, Jacen, and Lowbacca were together in a small, nondescript room. Jaina took a deep breath, scratched her straight brown hair, and ran her hands down her grease-smeared jumpsuit to make sure everything was still intact.

Suddenly recalling the attack on GemDiver Station, Jaina sat up so quickly that a fresh wave of nausea washed over her and pain exploded at her temples. She gasped, then forced herself to relax and let some of the pain drain away. "Where are we?" she asked.

Jacen was already sitting up on a narrow pallet, rubbing his brandy-brown eyes and running long fingers through his tousled hair. He wore a look of confusion, and Jaina sensed deep turmoil coming from her brother. "Not a clue," he said.

Lowbacca also made a dismayed, questioning sound.

"Least we're all together," Jaina said. "And they didn't put binders on us." She held up her hands, surprised that the Imperials had not separated their prisoners and tied them up. Water and a food tray lay in an alcove by the wall. From the looks of it, Lowie had already sampled some of the fruit.

"Hey, I wonder what happened to everyone at GemDiver Station. What do you suppose they did to Lando?" Jacen asked.

Jaina shrugged, still feeling queasy. "Saw him lying unconscious just before they stunned us. But I don't think they planned to kill him. They weren't looking for Corusca gems, either. Seems like they only wanted *the three of us.*"

"Yeah . . . kinda makes you feel valuable, huh?" Jacen agreed glumly. Lowie growled.

Jaina stood up and stretched, feeling better as she moved. "Guess I'm okay, though. How about you two?"

Jacen smiled reassuringly, and Lowie nodded

his shaggy head. The streak of black fur that swept over his eyebrows bristled with uneasiness. He smoothed the fur back and grunted.

It was then that Jaina noticed something else wrong. She looked down at the Wookiee's waist, but the miniaturized translating droid was no longer there.

"Lowie! What happened to Em Teedee?"

Lowie made a strange, sad sound and patted his waist.

"Imperials must've taken it from him," Jaina said. "What do they want?"

"Oh, just to take over the galaxy, cause a bunch of problems . . . hurt a lot of people—you know, the usual," Jacen answered flippantly. He went over to the flat metal door. "Hmmmm . . . it's probably locked, but there's no harm in trying," he said, tapping the controls with his fingers.

To Jaina's surprise, the door hummed sideways to reveal a guard standing at attention just outside. A stormtrooper in a skull-like white helmet turned to face them.

"Whoa!" Jacen cried, then he lowered his voice. "Well, at least the door opens."

"Maybe they just can't figure out how to lock the door," Jaina said. "Remember how clunky and unreliable Imperial technology is." She let sarcasm seep into her voice for the guard's benefit. "And you know how lousy stormtrooper armor is. Probably couldn't even stop a water blaster."

"Just walk past him," Jacen suggested in a stage

whisper, seeing that the stormtrooper hadn't moved. "Maybe he won't stop us."

The stormtrooper shouldered his blaster rifle. "Wait here." The filtered voice coming through the white helmet was flat, but somehow menacing. The guard spoke quietly into his helmet comlink, then shut the three young Jedi Knights in their cell again.

They sat in anxious silence for a moment. "We could tell jokes," Jacen suggested.

Before Jaina could think of an appropriate answer, the cell door whisked open again. This time, beside the stormtrooper stood the towering, sinister woman from the assault on GemDiver Station. Jaina took a quick breath.

The tall woman's black hair flowed like waves of darkness down her shoulders, and her ebony cape sparkled with bits of polished gems, swirling around her like a starry night sky. Her violet eyes blazed in a face so pale it seemed carved from polished bone. Her lips were a dark wine color, as if she had just eaten an overripe fruit. The woman was beautiful—in a cruel sort of way.

"So, Jedi Knights, you are awake at last," she snapped. Her voice was deep and thick, without the hissing edge Jaina had expected. "I must begin by saying how *disappointed* I am in you. I had hoped for more resistance from such powerful students already trained in the Force. Your Jedi defenses were pitiful! But we shall change that. You will be taught new ways. Effective ways."

The woman spun on one heel, and her black cloak swept around her like trailing smoke. "Follow me," she said, and stepped into the corridor.

"No," Jaina responded. "Who do you think you are? Why have you brought us here against our will?"

"I said *follow*!" the woman repeated. When they made no move to comply, she pointed her polished nails at them and twitched her fingers.

Suddenly, it felt as if a resilient invisible cord had wrapped around Jaina's throat. The woman crooked her finger, yanking at Jaina as if she were a pet on a leash. Jaina lurched as the invisible rope hauled her out of the cell.

Lowbacca and Jacen strained against similar bonds of Force, the Wookiee yowling his defiance. Despite their struggles, all three children were dragged on Force leashes tripping and stumbling into the corridor.

"I can do this all the way to the bridge, if you like," the woman said, her deep red lips curved into a mocking smile. "Or, you can save your energies for more productive resistance later."

"All right," Jaina croaked, sensing that this woman had dark Jedi powers she could not match—at least not yet.

When the Force bonds dropped away, the companions stood gasping and trembling. They looked at each other in angry humiliation, knowing they were beaten.

Jaina was the first to recover. Swallowing hard,

she stood straight, put her chin in the air, and followed the woman in black. Her brother and Lowie fell in behind Jaina. "Who are you?" Jaina asked after a while.

The woman paused in midstep, as if considering, then answered. "My name is Tamith Kai. I am from a new order of Nightsisters."

"Nightsisters? You mean like on Dathomir?" Jacen asked.

Jaina remembered the stories their friend Tenel Ka told when it was her turn to scare them before they practiced Jedi calming techniques—stories of the horrible evil women who had once twisted civilization on her world.

Tamith Kai looked at Jacen, her wine-dark lips set in something between a scowl and a smile. "You've heard of us? Good. My planet is rich in Force-wielders, and the Empire has helped to bring us back. Now perhaps you'll realize you can't resist. Cooperation, on the other hand, will be rewarded."

"We won't cooperate with you," Jaina challenged.

"Yes, yes," Tamith Kai said, as if bored. "All in good time."

"Hey, where are you taking us?" Jacen asked, walking quickly to keep pace with his sister. Lowie strode behind them, grumbling and fumbling at his waist as if he actually missed Em Teedee.

"You'll see soon enough," the Nightsister said. "We are almost ready to leave hyperspace."

All four of them stepped onto a lift platform that carried them up a level and opened out onto the bridge of the fleeing ship. The single pilot sat with his back to them in a padded high-backed chair, hunched over the controls. Ahead, through the bridge viewports Jaina could see the swirling colors of hyperspace.

The pilot reached out with his right hand and grabbed a lever as a countdown trickled to zero. Then he yanked the lever, and hyperspace suddenly unfolded, washing away into the star-studded darkness of normal space.

"We're near the Core Systems," Jaina said immediately, looking out at the rich starfields and the streamers of interstellar gas clotted together near the center of the galaxy.

The crowded Core Systems were the last bastions of Imperial power; not even New Republic forces had been able to flush them out completely. But they had arrived nowhere close to any system. They found themselves merely hanging, out in the middle of the star-strewn blackness.

"We have reached our destination, Tamith Kai," the pilot said, swiveling in his tall chair.

Jaina's heart leaped as she recognized the weary, hard-bitten face and iron-gray hair of the former TIE pilot who had been stranded on Yavin 4 for so many years.

"Qorl!" Jacen exclaimed.

Lowie roared in anger.

Qorl had attacked them in the jungles when the

young Jedi Knights had found his crashed TIE fighter and tried to fix it. The Imperial pilot had shot at Lowie and Tenel Ka, who had managed to escape into the undergrowth, but Qorl had taken Jacen and Jaina prisoner.

"Greetings, young friends. I never did thank you for fixing my ship and allowing me to return to my Empire."

"You betrayed us!" Jaina cried, feeling a surge of anger toward the brainwashed man. While being held captive, the twins had befriended Qorl, exchanging stories with him around the campfire. Jaina had felt sure the TIE pilot was softening, realizing that the ways of the Empire were filled with lies. But in the end, Qorl's military conditioning had been too strong.

"I returned as any soldier would and gave my report," Qorl said in a dull voice. "These people accepted me and . . . reindoctrinated me. I told them of your existence—powerful young Jedi Knights just waiting to be trained to serve the Empire."

"Never," Jaina and Jacen snapped in unison, and Lowbacca agreed with a roar.

Tamith Kai looked down at them mockingly. Standing beside Qorl, the dark-haired woman seemed even taller than before, more intimidating than ever. "Your anger is good," she said. "Fuel it. Let it grow. We will use it when your training begins. But for now . . . we have reached our destination."

Lowie gave a growl of disbelief.

Jaina looked out the front viewports, trying to calm herself. Master Skywalker had said that giving in to anger was a path to the dark side of the Force. She must not lash out, she knew; she must think of some other way to fight back.

"We're in the middle of empty space," Jaina said. "What is there for us to see?"

"Space is not always empty," Tamith Kai said. Her thick voice held a singsong quality, as if her mind was thinking of something else. "Reality is not always what it seems."

At his station Qorl verified the coordinates, then punched in a security code. "Transmitting now," he said.

Tamith Kai turned her sharp violet eyes toward the young Jedi Knights. "You are about to begin a new phase of your lives," she said, pointing to the viewscreens. "Behold."

Space shimmered like a blanket of invisibility peeling away. Suddenly a space station hung in front of them, torus-shaped, like a donut. Weapons emplacements ringed the station's entire perimeter, pointing in all directions, making it look like a spiked disciplinary collar for some ferocious beast. Tall observation towers rose like pinnacles on one side of the station.

Jaina swallowed hard.

"Cloaking device off," Qorl announced.

"Take a good look," Tamith Kai said, but she did not glance at the viewscreens. Her eyes glittered with violet fervor at the children. "Here you'll be trained as Dark Jedi . . . for the Empire."

Qorl spoke up, reminding her. "We must commence docking immediately and reactivate the invisibility shielding."

The Nightsister nodded but did not seem to hear, never taking her eyes off the young Jedi Knights. "Welcome to the Shadow Academy," she whispered.

7

TENEL KA SLID a hand under the crash webbing of the copilot's seat and scratched at the rough-woven, unfamiliar material of her disguise. She wished for the dozenth time that she could wear her comfortable reptilian armor, which was as supple as it was protective and never irritated her skin.

She had been silent, intimidated, through most of the journey to Borgo Prime, unable to bring herself to speak. Beside her sat Master Skywalker—the most famous and revered Jedi in the entire galaxy—calmly and competently piloting the *Off Chance*, an old blockade runner Lando had won in a sabacc game and claimed he no longer needed.

Tenel Ka's grandmother had insisted that the girl's royal training include diplomacy and correct methods of addressing individuals of any rank, species, age, or gender. Though not loquacious, Tenel Ka was also not shy; yet somehow, alone with the impressive Jedi Master in the confines of their tiny cockpit, she could find nothing to say.

She tried to think, but her sluggish mind would not cooperate. Weariness clung to her like the sweat-damp clothing she wore. She squirmed in her seat and tried to suppress a nervous yawn.

Luke glanced over at her, a smile at the corners of his mouth. "Tired?"

"Not much sleep," Tenel Ka answered, embarrassed that he had noticed her fatigue. "Bad dreams."

Luke's blue eyes narrowed for a moment, as if he was searching for a memory, but then he shook his head. "I haven't been sleeping well either—but, tired or not, we can't afford to make mistakes. Let's go over our cover story again. Tell me who you are."

"We are traders from Randon. We will avoid using names. But, if we must, you are Iltar and I am your ward-cousin Beknit. We trade in archaeological treasures. We are not above breaking the law to make a profit. We have come from a secret archaeological dig on . . ." She paused for a moment, searching her brain for the name of the planet.

"Ossus," Luke supplied.

"Ah. Aha," Tenel Ka said. "Ossus." She took a deep breath while she etched the name into her mind, then she continued. "On *Ossus*, we discovered a treasured vault, secured with an Old Republic seal. The treasure chamber is set deep into rock and plated with armor so thick that no blaster or laser can pierce it.

"We dare not blast the surrounding rock for fear of destroying the treasure. We've come to Borgo Prime in search of industrial-grade Corusca gems to slice through the armor and open the treasure vault. We are ready to pay handsomely for the right type of gems."

Tenel Ka watched with interest as the dull, lumpy asteroid of Borgo Prime loomed in their forward viewports. The rock had been hollowed out, honeycombed in ages past by generations of asteroid miners who sought one type of mineral, then another as market conditions changed. But more than a century ago, Borgo Prime had been stripped clean of even the least-desirable ore—leaving a spongelike network of interlocked caves, fully equipped with all the life-support systems and transportation airlocks the miners had needed. It had been a simple matter to convert the played-out mine into a bustling spaceport.

Luke transmitted the standard request for clearance to land and received it without difficulty.

"We've been cleared for docking bay ninety-four," Luke said. "Are you ready, uh, Beknit?"

Tenel Ka nodded matter-of-factly. "Of course, Iltar."

Luke studied her for a moment, earnest concern filling his face. "It could be rough down there, you know. You heard what Lando said: Borgo Prime is filled with people who have no conscience—thieves, murderers, creatures who would just as soon kill you as greet you."

"Ah. Aha," Tenel Ka said, raising an eyebrow. "Sounds like a visit to my grandmother's court on Hapes."

The two Randoni traders, "Iltar" and his ward-cousin "Beknit," left their blockade runner in the dockyard cavern behind an immense hangar door and walked along the causeway that joined Borgo Prime's largest space dock to its business district deep in the core of the asteroid.

In spite of her many rehearsals, Tenel Ka found it difficult to remember that she was supposed to be an experienced trader, used to frequenting such spaceports. She gawked openly at the tall rows of prefabricated dwellings welded up and down the inner walls and all the garish flashing lights of the alien businesses in separate atmosphere domes around them.

This place was so different from the primitive, untamed world of Dathomir. Even Hapes with its serene and stately cities—some of them larger than this entire asteroid—bore no resemblance to the spaceport's seedy, gaudily lit establishments, that hummed with a life of their own. Overhead, through the clear arching plasteel that covered a rift in the ceiling, the stars and space were all but obscured by Borgo Prime's glaring lights.

Luke paused beside Tenel Ka, letting her collect her thoughts. "You've never been anyplace like this, have you?" he asked.

She shook her head and started to walk again,

searching for words to describe the unsettling emotions. "I feel . . . foolish. Out of place." She scuffed her toes along a causeway surface that was paved with colorful, glowing advertisements.

She paused to read an ad, then another. The first one announced in phosphorescent script that flared into light as she stepped near it,

BORGO LANDING
SPACE DOCKS BY THE HOUR OR BY THE MONTH.

The next one said simply

INFO TO GO
DISCREET INQUIRIES OF ALL SORTS
COMPLETELY CONFIDENTIAL.

Tenel Ka shook her head. "I do not understand this place," she said. "It both revolts and . . . entices me at the same time."

"You don't have to go through with this, you know," Luke said. "I could handle it myself."

It was completely true, Tenel Ka realized—an uncomfortable thought. She tossed her head and ran a nervous hand over her hair, which she wore loose, in Randoni style, so that it flowed down her back in a cascade of red-gold ripples like a sun-dappled stream. She tried to look confident, but icy fingers of doubt prodded her mind. "I will do what I must to rescue my friends," she said, her voice as brisk and businesslike as she could make it. "Where is this nest or hive that Lando told us to find?"

Luke pointed to another lighted ad at their feet. "I think we just found it," he said with a pleased expression.

The flat image showed an insectoid barkeeper proffering a dozen drinks with its multijointed, chitinous arms. A row of blinking beacon lights set into the walkway indicated the direction of the "hive."

A sudden bout of stage fright assailed Tenel Ka, but she knew how important it was for them to stay in character. She straightened her clothing, cleared her throat, and looked at Luke. "You must be very thirsty after your long journey, Iltar," she said.

"Yes. Thank you, Beknit," he answered smoothly. "I could use a drink." Then he leaned toward her and asked in a lower voice, "Are you *sure* you want to do this?"

Tenel Ka nodded firmly. "I'm ready for anything."

"I did not expect an establishment quite so large on an asteroid of this size," Tenel Ka said, tilting back her head to look at the rounded ripples of

Shanko's cone-shaped Hive, a gray-green edifice sealed in its own atmosphere field. The edifice rose at least a quarter kilometer above the inner floor of Borgo Prime.

Feathery wings of fear and uncertainty fluttered in her stomach, and she paused to draw in a deep breath. To Tenel Ka's great chagrin, a subtle spark of amusement danced in Master Skywalker's eyes. "You know what waits for us in there, don't you?" he asked.

"Thieves," she answered.

"Murderers," he added.

"Liars, scum, smugglers, traitors . . ." Her voice trailed off.

"Almost like family back on Hapes?" he asked with a gentle, teasing smile.

As heir to the Royal Throne of Hapes, Tenel Ka had faced trained assassins, as had her father, Prince Isolder, before her. If she could do that, surely she could handle a little spaceport cantina.

"Thank you," she said, taking the arm he offered. "I am ready now."

Luke slid a pass chit into a small slot in the door. "Let's try to keep a low profile." The door slid open.

The first thing that caught Tenel Ka's eye when she stepped through the door was the insectoid bartender, Shanko, who stood over three meters high.

The room was filled with indescribable odors she could not begin to identify—not actually pleasant, but not quite offensive either. Particulates hung in the air from a multitude of burning objects: pipes, candles, incense, chunks of peat in blazing bog-pits, even clothing or fur from the occasional customer who got too close to one of the fires.

Without speaking, Luke gestured with his chin toward the bar. Even if he had spoken aloud, Tenel Ka could not have heard him above the noise of at least half a dozen different bands playing hit tunes from as many different systems.

Fortunately, they had decided before entering where they should start their inquiries. Knowing that on Randon the female ward-cousin was highly honored—mainly for her potential inheritance—and was always served first, Tenel Ka stepped up to the bar to place her order.

"Welcome travelersssss," Shanko said, folding three pairs of multijointed arms and bowing until his antennaed head nearly touched the bar.

"Your hospitality is as welcome as the prospect of refreshment," Tenel Ka replied.

"Sssso, you have been well ssschooled," Shanko said. "Are you perhapsss a sssscholar? A diplomat?"

"She is my ward-cousin," Luke put in smoothly.

"Then it iss *indeed* an honor to ssserve you," Shanko said, raising himself to his full three-meter height.

"I would like a Randoni Yellow Plague," Tenel

Ka said without hesitation. "Chilled. Make it a double."

"And I would like a Remote Terminator," Luke said.

The covering membranes of the bartender's multifaceted eyes nictated twice in surprise. "Not often requesssted. A ssstrong drink, iss it not?" He seemed flustered for a moment, then made a gurgling buzz deep in his thorax that Tenel Ka could only interpret as a laugh. "Will that be preprogrammed or randomizzzed?"

"Randomized, of course," Luke replied.

"Ah, a rissssk taker," Shanko said, tapping two forelegs on the bartop in approval.

Then his arms became a blur of motion as he pulled levers and pushed buttons, filling cups and vials, mixing their drinks in less time than it had taken to order them.

"There is no profit without risk," Luke said, accepting his drink from one of Shanko's many hands.

Tenel Ka leaned forward and lowered her voice. "We seek information," she said, drawing out a small string of Corusca gems that she had kept hidden under the rough material of her robe until then.

Shanko nodded in understanding. "We have the finessst information brokerss in the Sssector. There iss even a Hutt." He gestured toward an area to the right of the bar. "If you do not find what you ssseek here," he said with obvious pride, "it isss not to be found on Borgo Prime."

They thanked Shanko and headed in the direction he had indicated. The music of the bands faded slightly as they pushed into the milling throng of patrons, each imbibing its favorite form of refreshment. The crowd was so thick, Tenel Ka could not see where they were going.

Beside her, Luke paused and closed his eyes. "A Hutt information broker, huh?" he mused aloud. "They're the best you can get."

Tenel Ka felt a slight tingle as she watched him reach out with the Force to touch the minds around him, searching. She searched, too, but with her gray eyes open. A quick glance revealed nothing of interest. She looked up the open center of the hive's cone and at the curving stairways that climbed its ridged sides, which—judging from the signs on the walls—led to gambling rooms and lodgings.

Luke opened his eyes. "Okay, I have him." He took Tenel Ka's arm and pushed his way through the crowd. They passed a bank of stim lights, where a cluster of photosensitive customers wriggled and bounded to silent strobing "music."

They found the Huttese information broker ensconced behind a low table near the wall of the hive. A small Ranat with gray-brown fur stood at the Hutt's elbow, whiskers twitching. The Hutt was thin by Huttese standards and could not have had much status on his homeworld. Perhaps that was why he did business on Borgo Prime, Tenel Ka thought.

"We have come for information, and we are prepared to pay for it," Luke said without preamble.

The Hutt picked up a small datapad that lay on the table in front of him and punched a few buttons.

"What are your names?" he asked.

"What is *your* name?" Tenel Ka asked, raising her chin slightly.

The Hutt's eyes narrowed to slits, and Tenel Ka had the impression that the broker was revising his opinion of them. "Of course," he said. "Such things are unimportant."

Luke shrugged. "And all information has its price."

"Of course," the Hutt repeated. "Please sit down and tell me what you need."

Luke sat on a repulsorbench, adjusted the height, and motioned for Tenel Ka to sit beside him, next to a planter holding a tall, leafy shrub. Luke took a long gulp from the drink in his hand, but when Tenel Ka raised her cup to her lips, he sent her a warning look. When the Hutt bent to confer with his Ranat assistant for a moment, Luke took the opportunity to whisper, "That drink could knock you from here to the Outer Rim."

"Ah," Tenel Ka said. "Aha." She set the drink down with a small *thunk*.

When the Ranat scurried off on whatever business the Hutt had assigned it, Luke and Tenel Ka began telling their fictional tale, carefully offering only as much information as they thought was needed.

As they rambled on, taking turns embellishing the details, the other patrons in the hive supplied the usual chaos of a busy, seedy bar. Several different blaster battles rang out from dim areas, while huge armored bouncer droids trundled in to bash heads together and eject any customers who did not pay for the messes they made.

A group of smugglers played a reckless game of rocket darts, missing the prominent target on the wall and launching one of the small flaming missiles into the side of a fluffy, white-furred Talz. The creature roared in pain and surprise as his fur ignited, then took out his misery on the drunken Ithorian sitting next to him.

Large customers tried to eat smaller customers, and the bands kept playing, and Shanko kept mixing drinks. The Hutt information broker was distracted by none of it.

As they spoke, Luke continued to sip his drink and Tenel Ka cast about for a way to dispose of hers. When the Ranat returned and conferred again with the Hutt, Tenel Ka reached over to the planter beside her chair and dumped half of her drink into it.

It was only after the stalk began to shudder violently and the leaves curled up that Tenel Ka realized that the shrub was not a decoration but a plant-alien customer! She whispered an apology and turned back just as the Ranat hurried off with the Hutt's datapad and a new assignment.

The Ranat came back in a moment, followed by a heavily bearded man who walked with a limp.

"This Ranat here said 'no names,' and that's fine with me," the bearded man said, sitting down at the table. "Ranat tells me yer in the market for an industrial-grade Corusca gem? Ain't no one else can arrange that fer ya. Industrial-grade gems . . . sooner er later they hafta come through me."

"Are you the purchasing agent, then?" Tenel Ka said without thinking.

The bearded man snorted. "How 'bout we jes say I'm a middleman."

Again, Luke explained as briefly as possible about the treasure vault on Ossus, and before long they had struck a deal to purchase one industrial-grade Corusca gem.

That done, Luke probed the middleman for information about who else might have bought industrial-grade gems. The man's eyes grew wary and distrustful. "No names—that's the bargain," he said stoutly.

Tenel Ka pulled off another string of the fine Corusca gems that hung around her neck and placed them on the table beside the payment she and Luke had already made for the large gem.

"Surely you understand our caution," Luke said. "We must know if there is anyone capable of stealing our treasure from us."

The middleman picked up the string of gems and looked them over carefully. "Can't tell ya much," he said in a low voice. "Last shipment o' big industrial gems, one person bought 'em all. Big order."

"Can you describe their ships, tell us what planet they came from?" Luke pressed.

The bearded middleman still did not look up. "Not much, actually. Never saw the ship she came on. All I know's she called herself a . . . a lady of the evenin' . . . er a daughter of darkness, er somethin' like that."

Tenel Ka caught her breath, and she felt Luke stiffen beside her. "You mean a—a *Nightsister*?" Tenel Ka asked with a quaver in her voice.

"Yeah, that was it! A Nightsister," the middle-man said. "Goofy name."

Luke's eyes met Tenel Ka's and held.

"Thank you, gentlemen," Luke said slowly. "If you're right, I'm afraid this 'Nightsister' may have taken some of our valuables already."

8

JACEN STOOD BEHIND Qorl's pilot chair, biting his lip. The Nightsister Tamith Kai loomed over them, powerful and threatening. He flashed a glance at Jaina, but he didn't think they could do anything to resist.

Not yet anyway.

Docking doors on the ring of the Shadow Academy eased open in the silence of space, exposing a dark cavernous bay rimmed with flashing yellow lights to guide Qorl's ship in. The Imperial pilot worked the controls with grim proficiency, and Jacen noticed that his damaged left arm—which had never properly healed when his TIE fighter had crashed on Yavin 4—was now bulkier, encased in black leather from the shoulder down, wrapped with straps and battery packs.

"Qorl, what happened to your arm?" Jacen asked. "Did they heal it for you, like we promised we'd do at the Jedi academy?"

Qorl diverted his attention from the docking maneuvers, turning his haunted pale eyes toward the boy. "They did not heal it," Qorl said. "They *replaced* it. I now have a droid arm, which is better than my old one. Stronger, capable of more tasks." He bent his leather-bound arm.

Jacen caught the faint whirring of servomotors. His stomach clenched in sick revulsion. "They didn't have to do that," Jacen said. "We could have healed you in a bacta tank, or a medical droid could have tended you. At worst you would have been fitted with a biomechanical prosthetic that looks just like a real arm—even my uncle has one of those. There was no need to give you a droid arm."

Qorl's face was stony, and he turned his attention back to piloting his craft. "Nevertheless, it is done. My arm is better now, stronger."

The Imperial ship drifted into the docking bay, and lines of pulsing lights continued to illuminate the reflective metal walls. A transparisteel-encased observation bay with angular windows protruded from the inner wall above. Jacen could see small figures running diagnostics, working systems to guide Qorl's ship in.

The ship settled down with barely a bump. The docking-bay doors closed behind them, sealing the prisoners inside the sinister Shadow Academy.

Tamith Kai spoke into the comm channel. "Engage cloaking device," she said, her deep voice as irresistible and compelling as a tractor beam.

Though Jacen could see or feel nothing different, he knew that the large space station had suddenly vanished, leaving the illusion of nothing but empty space, where no one would ever find them.

Flanked by a stormtrooper escort, Tamith Kai ushered the children down the boarding ramp, away from the assault ship that had kidnapped them from GemDiver Station. She took them across the bay, toward a broad scarlet door that slid open as they approached.

On the other side stood a young-looking man dressed in flowing silvery robes. His smooth skin and silken blond hair seemed to glow. He was one of the most *beautiful* humans Jacen had ever seen— perfectly formed, like a holo simulation of an ideal man, or a sculptor's masterpiece chiseled out of alabaster. A contingent of stormtroopers stood behind him, blaster rifles resting on their shoulders.

"Welcome, new recruits," he said in a gentle voice that carried undertones of music. "I am Brakiss, leader of the Shadow Academy."

Jacen heard his sister gasp and couldn't restrain his own exclamation. "Brakiss?" he said. "Blaster bolts! We've heard about you. You were an Imperial spy planted at Master Skywalker's academy, trying to steal our training methods."

Brakiss smiled as if inwardly amused.

"That's right," Jaina continued excitedly. "Master Skywalker figured out who you were, but when he tried to turn you to the light side—to *save* you—you couldn't face the ugliness inside yourself."

Brakiss's smile never faltered. "Ah, so that's how he tells it? Master Skywalker and I did not agree on the . . . particulars of training in the Force. But he had at least one good idea: He was correct to bring back the Jedi Knights. He realized that the Jedi were the preservers and protectors of the Old Republic. They unified the decaying old government and kept it alive long after it should have dissolved into anarchy.

"And now that there is anarchy among the remnants of the Imperial forces, *we* need such a unifying force. We have already found a powerful new leader, a great one"—Brakiss smiled—"but we also need our own group of Dark Jedi Knights, Imperial Jedi, who will cement our factions together and give us the will to defeat the wicked and unlawful government of the New Republic and bring about the Second Imperium."

"Hey, our *mother* leads the New Republic!" Jacen objected. "She's not wicked. And she doesn't torture people, or kidnap them, either."

Brakiss said, "It all depends on your perspective."

"Who's this new leader, anyway?" Jaina interrupted. "Haven't you tried to find a single leader before—and ended up with everyone fighting to run what's left of the Empire? It won't work."

"Silence," Tamith Kai said, her voice thick with menace. "You will not ask questions; you will receive indoctrination. You will be trained as powerful warriors to fight in the service of the Empire."

"I don't think so," Jacen said defiantly.

His sister's face flushed with anger. "We won't cooperate with you. You can't steal us away and just expect us to be diligent little students for you. Master Skywalker and our parents will comb the galaxy to find us. They *will* find us, and then you'll be sorry."

Behind them, Lowie snarled and spread his long arms as if longing to tear something limb from limb, as his uncle Chewbacca was rumored to do whenever he lost a hologame.

The stormtroopers suddenly trained their rifles on the infuriated Wookiee.

"Hey, don't shoot him!" Jacen said, moving between the stormtrooper and Lowie.

Jaina spoke up in an authoritative tone that took Jacen by surprise. "What have you done with Em Teedee, Lowie's translator droid? He needs to communicate—unless of course all of these stormtroopers can somehow speak the Wookiee language?"

"He will be given his little droid back," Tamith Kai said, "as soon as it has undergone . . . suitable reprogramming."

Brakiss clapped his hands at the troopers. "We will go to their quarters now," he said. "Their training must begin soon. The Second Imperium has a great need for Dark Jedi Knights."

"You'll never turn us," Jaina said. "You're wasting your time."

Brakiss looked at her, smiled indulgently, and stood in silence for a long moment. "You may find that your mind will change," he said. "Why don't we wait and see."

The stormtroopers formed an armed escort around them as they marched along the clanking metal deck plates.

The Shadow Academy was not comfortable and soft like Lando's GemDiver Station. The walls were not painted with pastel colors; there were no soothing strains of music or nature sounds over the loudspeaker systems, only harsh status reports and chronometer tones that chimed every quarter hour. Stenciled labels marked the doors. Occasional computer terminals mounted to the walls displayed maps of the station and complicated simulations in progress.

"This is an austere station," Tamith Kai said as Jacen stared at the cold, heartless walls. "We don't bother with luxury accommodations like your jungle academy. However, we have made sure that you each have a private chamber so you can conduct your meditation exercises, practice your assignments, and concentrate on developing your Force skills."

"No!" Jaina said.

"We'd rather stay together," Jacen added.

Lowbacca roared in agreement.

Tamith Kai came to an abrupt stop and looked down at them. "I did not *ask* your preference!" she said, her violet eyes blazing. "You will do as you are told."

They reached an intersection of corridors, and here they split into three groups. Brakiss led the cluster of stormtroopers that surrounded Jaina, taking them down a corridor to the right. A larger group of guards, tense and with weapons at the ready, helped Tamith Kai to escort Lowbacca. The remaining guards closed around Jacen and led him off to the left.

"Wait!" Jacen cried, and turned to look at his twin sister for what felt to him like the last time. Jaina stared back at him, her brandy-brown eyes wide with anxiety, but when she bravely lifted her chin, Jacen felt a surge of courage himself. They would find some way out of this.

The guards hustled him down a long corridor until they stopped at one door in a line of identical-seeming doors. Student chambers, he thought.

The door whisked open, and the stormtroopers herded Jacen into a small cubicle, bare-walled and uncomfortable. He saw no speaker panel on the wall, no controls, nothing that would let him communicate with anybody.

"I'm staying in here?" he said in disbelief.

"Yes," the lead stormtrooper said.

"But what if I need something? How am I supposed to call out?" Jacen said.

The trooper turned his skull-like plasteel mask to look directly at him. "Then you will *endure* until someone comes for you." The stormtroopers stepped back, and the door shut behind Jacen, closing him in, weaponless and alone.

Then, to make things worse, all the lights went out.

9

TENEL KA WOKE to pitch-darkness, cramped and confined, surrounded by a dull vibration. Her heart drummed a rapid cadence, and perspiration prickled her skin. An urgency, a feeling that something was terribly wrong, nudged the back of her mind. She tried to sit up and bumped her head— hard—against the unyielding bottom of the bunk above her. Stifling an exclamation of annoyance, she remembered that she was aboard the *Off Chance*. She relaxed slightly—but only slightly.

When they had finished with the Hutt information broker on Borgo Prime, Luke and Tenel Ka decided their best hope for finding Jacen, Jaina, and Lowbacca lay in going directly to Dathomir, homeworld of the original Nightsisters. Their only clue was the mysterious Nightsister, and they had to find out who she was and whether she had the twins and Lowbacca.

Luke had urged Tenel Ka to get some sleep while they made their journey. It was the first opportunity she had had to rest since her friends had been kidnapped, and Tenel Ka gratefully accepted.

And so she had slept, sealed away from light and sound, in one of the berths aboard the *Off Chance*, but her rest had again been disturbed by shadowy dreams. She touched a switch by her head and winced as bright cabin light flooded the sleeping cubicle. She rolled onto her stomach, swung her legs over the side of the bunk, and dropped a meter and a half to the floor of the cabin. Shaking back her tumble of loose red-gold hair, Tenel Ka stretched to her full height and noted with pleasure the freedom of movement that her tough, supple lizard-hide armor afforded her. She was glad to be dressed as a warrior again.

The uneasy feeling left by her dream persisted as Tenel Ka made her way to the cockpit and lowered herself into the copilot's seat next to Luke. She gazed through the front viewport at the swirling colors that indicated the *Off Chance* was traveling through hyperspace.

Luke looked up from the controls. "Did you get some sleep?"

"This is a fact." She fastened the crash webbing around her, then grabbed a thick clump of her hair and began plaiting it into a braid, adding a few feathers and beads that she kept in a pouch attached to her belt.

"But you didn't sleep *well*?"

She blinked at this, somehow surprised that he had noticed. "This is also a fact."

Luke did not reply. He simply waited, and with growing discomfort she realized he was waiting for her to explain.

"I . . . had a dream," she said. "It is not important."

His intense blue eyes searched her face. When he spoke, it was in a low voice. "I feel fear in you."

She grimaced and shrugged. "It is a dream I have had before."

His eyelids fluttered shut briefly, and he tilted his head as he might have done had he been studying her with his eyes open. ". . . the Nightsisters?" he said at last.

"Yes. It is childish," she admitted as color rushed to her cheeks, staining them with embarrassment.

"Strange . . . I dreamt about them, too," Luke said.

Tenel Ka looked at him in disbelief. "I used to think they were just a story that mothers and grandmothers on Dathomir told to scare children. But the Nightsisters were all destroyed. How could there be any left?"

"The people of Dathomir are often strong in the Force, and it would not be difficult for someone else to train them in the ways of evil," he said. He leaned back in the pilot's seat and stared out at hyperspace as if summoning an old memory. "In fact, many years ago—before you were born—I traveled to Dathomir searching for Jacen and Jaina's parents, Han and Leia. That was when I met your mother and father, and we all joined forces to defeat the last of the Nightsisters."

Tenel Ka looked at him curiously. This was a part of the story her parents spoke little about. "My mother thinks very highly of you," she said, hoping he would elaborate.

Luke slid her a teasing glance. "But did she ever tell you how we met? That she *captured* me?"

"You don't mean—" Tenel Ka began. "She couldn't have expected . . ."

Luke chuckled at her discomfiture. "This is a fact."

"Oh, Master Skywalker!" Tenel Ka gasped in chagrin at the very idea of Luke submitting to the primitive marriage customs she had always viewed as quaint and provincial. On Dathomir, a woman selected and captured the man she wanted to marry. Her mother, Teneniel Djo, had done *that* to Luke Skywalker?

It brought a renewed flush of embarrassment to her face to realize that her mother had captured the greatest Jedi Master in the galaxy and had expected him to marry her and father her children. Then, all at once, the situation struck her as so ridiculous that she let loose with what was, for her, a rare sound indeed—a giggle.

"My mother has always taught me to have respect for Jedi, and most of all for you, Master Skywalker, but . . . please do not be offended"— she gasped, tears of mirth rising to her eyes—"I am certainly glad she did not succeed."

Luke, still smiling, reached over and gave her shoulder an understanding squeeze. "So am I. Your parents belonged together."

"I love my father, you know," Tenel Ka said, sobering, "and my mother."

"And yet you've never told your friends who your real parents are," Luke said. "Why?"

Tenel Ka squirmed uncomfortably in her crash restraints, which suddenly felt too confining. She had often mulled this problem over, and had come to the same decision again and again. "It is difficult to explain," she said. "I am not ashamed of my parents, if that is what you think. I am proud that my mother is strong in the Force and that she, a warrior from Dathomir, now rules the entire Hapes Cluster. And I am proud of my father and what he managed to become, despite the way he was raised—despite the one who raised him."

Luke nodded sagely. "Your grandmother?"

"Yes," Tenel Ka gritted. "Of *that* part of my family, I am not proud. My grandmother is power-hungry. She manipulates. I am not sure she even knows how to love." She felt a bleak bewilderment as she turned to look at Luke. "Yet my father is loving and wise. He is not like her."

"No, he isn't," Luke said. "Long ago your father Isolder did something difficult and very brave. Realizing that your grandmother loved power so much she was willing to kill anyone who threatened her, he rejected her teaching. She is a strong, proud woman, but her lessons were poisonous.

He chose instead to value and honor life wherever he found it. Your father's difficult decision was the right one."

Tenel Ka nodded. Her thoughts were bitter. "My lineage is tainted by generations of bloodthirsty, power-hungry tyrants. I am not *proud* that I was born to the royal family of Hapes," she spat. "I do not wish my friends to know that I am heir to the throne, because I have done nothing to earn it, choose it, or deserve it."

Luke's face was thoughtful. "Jacen and Jaina would understand that. Their mother is one of the most powerful women in the galaxy."

Tenel Ka shook her head violently. "Before I tell them, I must prove to myself that I am not like my ancestors. I choose to take pride only in what *I* accomplish, first through my own strength, and then through the Force—never through inherited political power. My parents are very proud that I have decided to become a Jedi."

"I understand," Luke said. "You've chosen a difficult path." He smiled at her warmly. "It is a good start for a Jedi."

10

THE NEXT DAY, Jaina's joy at seeing her brother again was overshadowed by Tamith Kai's presence and the fact that they were each being shepherded down the corridor by a pair of well-armed stormtroopers.

When Jacen broke away from his guards just long enough to give her a quick hug, she spoke her words in a whispered burst. "I've got a plan. I need your help."

Rough, armored hands pulled the brother and sister apart. One of the armor-clad guards leveled his blaster pistol at the twins and motioned them to move on.

Jaina smiled in wry amusement. Even with Tamith Kai present, Brakiss still wasn't certain of their cooperation. The stormtroopers were here to ensure that they caused no trouble.

A slight nod of Jacen's head told Jaina that he understood her words. "Want to hear a joke?" he asked brightly, purposely changing the subject.

"Sure," Jaina answered with feigned innocence.

Jacen cleared his throat. "How many stormtroopers does it take to change a glowpanel?"

Jaina cringed inwardly. Her brother certainly was brave—or perhaps foolhardy. Nonetheless, she took the bait. "I don't know, how many stormtroopers *does* it take to change a glowpanel?"

One of the guards stepped ahead of Jaina and stopped at the door to a lecture room in which she could see dozens of people seated. She guessed they were probably the other Shadow Academy trainees. The guard with the blaster pistol gestured for them to enter.

"It takes two stormtroopers to change a glowpanel," Jacen said in a voice loud enough for everyone to hear. "One stormtrooper to change it, and the other one to shoot him and take credit for all the work."

Jaina tried unsuccessfully to suppress a snort of laughter. Tamith Kai glared violet daggers at Jacen.

Jacen squirmed under her angry regard and muttered, "I can tell *you're* from Dathomir. Your people aren't exactly known for their sense of humor."

As her two guards took her arms in a bruising grip, Jaina was forced to admit that her brother's small act of bravado had released something inside her, had shown her that her mind—at least for now—was still free, that she still had choices.

She was dragged into the meeting room, where her guards shoved her into a sitting position at

one end of a narrow, backless bench. Jacen's
guards seated him on the opposite side of the
room—no doubt to punish him for his joke. Jaina
was delighted to see that Lowie sat less than a
meter away from her, with only one student
between them. He roared a greeting at her and
Jacen.

The other students were all human, clean cut,
and wearing dark uniforms. They seemed eager to
learn, glad to be at the Shadow Academy, genuine
Imperial youth. She had seen people like this
before. She, Jacen, and Lowie might be the only
ones resisting the training, she knew.

Jaina frowned when she saw that Em Teedee
was still not at Lowie's belt. That would make
communication difficult. She wondered what her
uncle Luke would do in such a situation. She sat
up straight, cleared her mind, and sent a gentle
thought probing in Lowie's direction. She did not
feel any pain from him. He was unharmed—of
that she was certain—but she did sense tension,
confusion, and simmering frustration. She tried
to send him soothing thoughts. She wasn't sure
how much got through, but when Lowie briefly
reached a furry hand around to touch her shoulder, she knew he understood.

Jaina wondered if she dared speak openly to her
Wookiee friend. She would have to find out what
the student next to her was like first. He was
about her age, and a little taller. Like all the
willing students, he wore a tight, sleek-fitting

charcoal jumpsuit beneath a flowing robe of purest black. He had blond hair and moss-green eyes, and he glanced at her without any particular recognition or interest.

She sent her thought probe toward the young man, but caught nothing beyond elusive snatches that blared fleetingly in her mind, like disconnected notes from an orchestra tuning its instruments.

"Why are we here?" Jaina asked in a voice just above a whisper.

"Because we are here," he replied, aloof and a bit defensive. "Because Master Brakiss wishes us to be here." He looked at her with suspicion, as if she had proved herself mentally deficient. "Are we not all here to learn the ways of the Force from Master Brakiss?"

Before Jaina could reply, Brakiss himself strode into the chamber. The silence in the room was instant and complete. Not a cough or a syllable challenged his compelling presence. Brakiss let his piercing eyes rove across the faces of the gathered students. When his eyes met hers, Jaina felt an inexplicable chill creep down her spine.

Without preamble, he began to teach.

"The Force is an energy that surrounds all living things. It flows through us. It flows from us."

As his voice streamed around the students, Jaina felt her mind begin to relax. This wasn't so bad after all. All of it was true. The power in Brakiss's voice urged action, demanded agreement. Jaina saw the heads of many of the students nodding. She nodded too.

Jaina could not remember the words as Brakiss led them smoothly, logically from one concept to another. All she remembered were the thoughts, the feelings, the *rightness* of it all.

Then suddenly, for some reason—perhaps it was the light touch of a furry hand on her back— the words came into focus again, began to penetrate the complacent fog of unquestioning agreement that had blanketed her mind.

"You each have the tools inside you to master yourselves, and to master the Force," the tranquil, confident voice said. "And to draw on the strength of the Force, you must learn to draw on what is strongest in you: strong emotions, deep desires, fear, aggression, hate, anger."

A resounding *No!* rang through Jaina's mind, and she shook her head to clear it. "That . . . can't be true," she whispered. "It's not true."

The student next to Jaina flicked his eyes at her with a look of disdain. "Of *course* it's true," he said, as if using indisputable logic. "Master Brakiss said it, so it must be true."

"What makes you so sure?" Jaina hissed. "Can't you see that he has a hold on your mind? You should get away from this place and start thinking for yourself."

"I don't *wish* to leave," he said, his expression implacable. "I wish to study with Master Brakiss and become a Jedi."

Jaina seethed at his stubbornness. "Have you even thought about this? You can't just blindly accept whatever he says without bothering to think about it. What if he's wrong?"

"He is the *teacher*." The student's moss-green eyes blinked at her as if her question made no sense. He stood abruptly, begging Brakiss's attention.

Jaina took the opportunity to lean behind him and whisper to Lowie. "I've got a plan! In a couple of days, I'll need you to knock out all the station's power. Be ready." As she sat back up, her mind finally registered the fact that the stubborn blond student was addressing Brakiss.

"—is trying to convince your other students that they should not believe you, that you do not have the true teachings of the Force. And therefore I suggest that this—this *girl* is not a worthy pupil for you, Master Brakiss."

Brakiss's beautiful, piercing eyes narrowed and came to rest on Jaina. She felt the press of his powerful mind against hers. She tried to resist.

"You are new here," he said. "You do not know our ways. Listen to my teachings, then make your judgment. Decide for yourself. But do not encourage others to disbelieve me *ever* again."

In unison, the students murmured their agreement—with three exceptions.

"At this academy we do not learn only one side of the Force," Brakiss went on, resuming his lecture, though his comments seemed directed primarily toward Jacen, Jaina, and Lowie. "This is not a school of darkness. I call this a Shadow Academy, for what does life create by its very nature, if not shadows? And it is only through using the full range of your emotions and desires— the light *and* the dark—that you will become truly strong in the Force and fulfill your destiny. The light side by itself offers only limited power. But when the light is blended with the dark, and you work within the shadows, then you achieve your full potential. Use the strength of the dark side."

Jaina looked across at Jacen, who was slowly shaking his head. Close beside her, Lowie growled deep in his throat. Unable to contain herself any longer, Jaina stood. "That's not right," she said. "The dark side doesn't make you any stronger. It's faster, easier, more seductive. It's also more tenacious. Just as the light side brings freedom, the dark side brings only bondage. Once you enslave yourself to the dark side of the Force, you may never escape."

A collective gasp went up, but no one said a word as Jaina and Brakiss faced each other over the students' heads. Brakiss was silent for a long moment, his mind pressing down on hers with suffocating weight.

With a mental heave Jaina flung aside the influence of his mind on hers and challenged him, her eyes filled with pride, her thoughts free.

At last, Brakiss shook his head sadly. "I did not wish to make an example of you. But you leave me no choice. You have chosen to pit your puny light-side powers against my own. I gave you one warning. You will not receive another."

With that, Brakiss lifted one hand slightly, almost as if to wave a fond farewell. Blue fire danced from his fingertips and surrounded Jaina in a haze of bright agony.

Brakiss's calm cruelty against Jaina launched Lowbacca into an unbridled rage. Unable to control himself, he leaped from his cramped seat, knocking over the blond student. He howled at the top of his lungs and bared long Wookiee fangs. Ginger-colored fur stuck out in all directions as he yanked up the bench he had been sitting on and raised it over his head.

Alerted by the disturbance, the guards charged into the room, their stun pistols drawn, looking for the source of the chaos—and the enraged Wookiee was not difficult to find.

Lowie threw the bench at the incoming stormtroopers. His blow knocked the first cluster of guards backward into each other, tumbling them down like children's blocks. Five more stormtroopers tripped over their fallen companions but still managed to wade into the room.

The other Shadow Academy trainees added to the uproar, trying to shout Lowie down. The Wookiee just roared back at them. From the podium, Brakiss urged everyone to be calm, but no one listened.

Another door whisked open, and a new contingent of stormtroopers rushed in from the far side of the room.

Jacen dashed to his unconscious sister's side and cradled her head and shoulders in his lap. With relief, he sensed that she was not seriously injured from the Force blast. She groaned and blinked her brandy-brown eyes, trying to fight her way back to consciousness.

"Jaina," he called. "Jaina, snap out of it!"

"All right . . . I am," she said, struggling to sit up. Then she seemed suddenly to notice the brawl that Lowie had started on her behalf.

The second set of stormtroopers drew their stun pistols as Lowie yanked a bench out from under another Shadow Academy student, sending her to the floor. The student squealed in outrage. Lowie ignored her and raised the bench to throw at the incoming stormtroopers.

They pointed their stun pistols and fired— but the beam caught the front of the bench, doing no damage. Lowie tossed it, and the troopers scrambled out of the way as the bench crashed against the side wall. Lowbacca ducked to pick up something else to throw—and just as he did, the first set of stormtroopers on the other side of the room, finally climbing back to their feet, fired their stun pistols.

Glowing blue arcs shot over Lowie's back, missing him and striking full against three of the second set of troopers on the other side, stunning them. They sprawled senseless on the floor in a clattering tumble of white plasteel armor.

"Cease this disturbance!" Brakiss shouted. His normally smooth features had lost their serene composure.

One of the stormtroopers in the first group took two steps forward and aimed his stun pistol directly at Lowie's back as the Wookiee stood up, presenting an easy target.

Jacen watched and—in the moment before the stormtrooper could fire—used his greatest strength with the Force to grasp the trooper's blaster and wrench it halfway around, twisting it in the white-gloved hand so that when the guard squeezed the firing button, the barrel was pointed toward his own chest. The stun beam splashed out, knocking the trooper to the ground, unconscious.

"Lowie, I'm all right," Jaina called, picking herself up and climbing to her feet. "Look, I'm all right!"

More stormtroopers rushed in from both sides of the room, weapons drawn.

"Lowie, calm down," Jacen said.

Lowbacca looked from side to side, fingers spread, arms ready to tear something apart, until he saw he was clearly outnumbered.

Brakiss stood with his fingers outstretched. A shimmering power curled between them, ready to be unleashed.

"We don't want to damage you," Brakiss said,

filled with savage intensity, "but you must learn discipline." The master of the Shadow Academy looked to the stormtroopers. "Return them to their quarters, and keep them separated! We have great work to do here and cannot be distracted by unchanneled displays of temper."

Then Brakiss adjusted his handsome features until he looked calm and soothing again. He raised his eyebrows in admiration toward Lowie. "I am pleased to see the strength in your anger, young Wookiee. That is something we must develop. You have great potential."

White-armored guards crushed Lowie's hairy arms in their unfeeling grip. The stormtroopers marched the three young Jedi Knights out into the corridor and toward their cells.

11

DATHOMIR SPARKLED LIKE a rich topaz jewel, welcoming Tenel Ka as Luke piloted the *Off Chance* down into the atmosphere. Anticipation tingled through her. Regardless of the unhappy circumstances that brought them here, Tenel Ka could not help the feeling of pleasure and joy that throbbed through her veins with every beat of her heart. *Home-home. Home-home.*

Turbulence buffeted the blockade runner as they descended. Luke studied the displays on the navigation console and adjusted their course from time to time.

"It's been a long time since I made a visit to the Singing Mountain Clan," Luke said. "I don't remember exactly how to get there. I think I can get us close, but unless you happen to know the coordinates—"

Tenel Ka rattled off the numbers before he could finish his thought. At the same time, she leaned forward and entered the coordinates into the navicomp.

"I come here often," she explained. "It is my second home in the galaxy, but it is the first home of my heart."

"Yes," Luke said, "I can understand that."

As the *Off Chance* carried them to the home of the Singing Mountain Clan, they passed over shining oceans, lush forests, vast deserts, rolling hills, and wide fertile plains. Tenel Ka felt strength and energy flow through her, as if the very atmosphere of the planet had the power to recharge her.

"Look," Luke said, pointing down at a herd of blue-skinned reptiles racing at incredible speed across a plain.

"Blue Mountain people," Tenel Ka said. "They migrate every dawn and every dusk."

Luke nodded. "One of them gave me a ride once."

"That is a rare honor, Master Skywalker," she said. "Not even I have had that opportunity."

The pale pink sun was high above the horizon by the time they reached the wide, bowl-shaped valley of the Singing Mountain Clan, Tenel Ka's second home. A green and brown patchwork of fields and orchards spread beneath them in the pinkish sunlight. Small clusters of thatched huts dotted the valley, and morning cooking fires glimmered here and there.

Luke pointed to the stone fortress built into the

side of the cliff wall that rose high above the valley floor. "Does Augwynne Djo still rule here?"

"Yes. My great-grandmother."

"Good. We'll go directly to her then. I'd prefer to tell only a few people why we are here and keep our presence as secret as possible," he said, then he brought the *Off Chance* to a smooth landing on the valley floor beside the fortress.

"That should not be difficult," Tenel Ka replied. "My people do not speak unnecessarily."

Luke chuckled. "I can believe that."

Tenel Ka paused halfway up the steep path that led to the fortress. She was not at all fatigued; she was simply savoring the moment.

Luke, who had been following behind her with unwavering steps, halted without a word and waited for her to continue. He did not seem the least bit winded, his breathing slow and regular— no small feat considering the rapid pace Tenel Ka set.

The longer she knew Master Skywalker, the more she admired him, and the better she under- stood why her mother—who did not often speak highly of any man except her husband, Isolder— had always held Luke Skywalker in high esteem.

Tenel Ka drew in a deep breath. The air was delicious, but not just from the mouthwatering odors of roasting meat and vegetables that wafted from the cooking fires. It was late summer in the valley, and the warm breeze was redolent with the scents of ripening fruit, golden grasses, and early harvest. Despite the intermingled odors of the lizard pens and the herd of domesticated rancors, there was a freshness to the air that lifted her heart.

Tenel Ka set off again as if there was not a moment to lose. Finally, she stood before the gate of the fortress, where she announced herself as a member of the clan.

The gates were thrown open and Tenel Ka's clan sisters welcomed her with warm embraces and low murmurs of greeting. All were dressed in lizard-skin tunics of various colors, like the one Tenel Ka wore. Some wore elaborate helmets, while others simply wore their hair in decorated braids.

One clan sister with black hair that fell to her waist drew the two travelers inside. "Augwynne told us you would come," she said. Her expression was grave, but Tenel Ka could see the smile that lit her eyes.

"Our mission is urgent," Tenel Ka stated, not bothering to greet the woman. "We *must* see Augwynne alone at once." She had never used such a tone of command in Master Skywalker's presence before, but she knew her clan sister would not be offended. At times like this, pleasantries were an unnecessary luxury among her people.

The woman inclined her head slightly. "Augwynne has guessed this much. She waits for you in the war room."

The ancient woman stood as they entered the room. "Welcome, Jedi Skywalker. And welcome great-granddaughter Tenel Ka Chume Ta' Djo." She embraced each of them in turn.

Tenel Ka groaned. "Please," she said, "do not use my full name. And do *not* send word that we are here."

Luke interrupted. "We're following a trail that has led us from Yavin to Borgo Prime to Dathomir. Our need for information has brought us to you."

Tenel Ka took a deep breath and searched for words. She looked directly at her great-grandmother. Augwynne's wrinkle-nested eyes were attentive, cautious. "We are searching for the Nightsisters. Do any remain on Dathomir?"

Augwynne's heavy sigh told Tenel Ka that they had come to the right place. The old woman fixed her gaze on Luke. "They are not Nightsisters as you and I knew them," she said. "Not wizened crones with discolored skin, who rotted from the nightspells they spoke." She shook her head. "No, they are a newly formed order of Nightsisters, young and fair, and allied with the Empire." She lifted a finger to stroke Tenel Ka's cheek. "Their evil is subtle. They tame and ride rancors as we do. They dress as warriors, if they choose. They are not even all women . . . but they *are* the children of darkness. They are dangerous, with new goals. Do not seek them out."

"We must," Tenel Ka said simply. "It is our best hope for rescuing my closest friends."

Augwynne gave her great-granddaughter a measuring look. "You pledged friendship with these people you must rescue?"

Tenel Ka nodded. "With full ceremony."

"Then we have no other choice," Augwynne said with finality. "You must present your case before the Council of Sisters."

12

BRAKISS HAD A private office on the Shadow Academy, a place where he could go for solitude and contemplation.

Now, as he pondered, he stared at the brilliant images surrounding him on the walls: a waterfall of scarlet lava on the molten planet Nkllon; an exploding sun that spewed arcs of stellar fire in the Denarii Nova; the still-blazing core of the Cauldron Nebula, where seven giant stars had all gone supernova at once; and a vista of the broken shards of Alderaan, destroyed by the Empire's first Death Star more than twenty years before.

Brakiss recognized great beauty in the violence of the universe, in the unbridled power provided by the galaxy or unleashed by human ingenuity.

Standing alone and in silence, Brakiss used Force techniques to meditate and absorb these cosmic catastrophes, crystallizing the strength within himself. Through the dark side, he knew how to make the Force bend to his will. The power stored within the galaxy was his to use.

When he captured it and held it with his heart, Brakiss could maintain his calm exterior and not be prone to violence, as his fellow instructor Tamith Kai so often was.

Brakiss eased back in his padded chair, letting his breath flow slowly out. The synthetic leather squeaked as his body rubbed against it, and the warmers inside the chair brought the temperature to a relaxing level. The cushions conformed themselves to his body to give him the greatest comfort.

Tamith Kai refused such indulgences outright. She was a hard woman, insisting on privation and adversity to hone her skills for the Empire that had recognized her potential and taken her from the bleak planet Dathomir. Brakiss, however, found that he could *think* better when he was at ease. He could plan, mull over possibilities.

Brakiss switched on the recording pad on his desktop and called up the day's records. He would have to make a report and ship it in an armored hyperdrone to their powerful new Imperial leader, hidden deep in the Core Systems.

It had been some time since the encampment he founded in the Great Canyon on Dathomir had provided any strong new students, but the three talented young trainees kidnapped from Skywalker's Jedi academy were another story, worth the risk of stealing them. Brakiss could sense it.

But their focus was all wrong. Master Skywalker had taught them too much and in the wrong ways. They didn't know how to turn their anger into a sharpened spearpoint for a larger weapon. They contemplated too much. They were too calm, too passive—except for the Wookiee. Brakiss needed to train those three. He and Tamith Kai would employ their separate specialties to work on them.

Brakiss drummed his fingertips on the slick surface of his desk. Occasionally, he felt twinges of sadness for having left the Yavin 4 training center. He had learned much there, though his own mission for the Empire was always uppermost in his mind.

Long ago, the Empire had selected Brakiss because of his untapped Jedi ability. He had undergone rigorous training and conditioning so that he could spy on Skywalker's academy, gathering precious information. No one was supposed to know he was a scout, planted there to learn techniques that he could teach to the Second Imperium. The new Imperial leader had insisted on developing his own Dark Jedi, a symbol that those faithful to the Empire could rally around.

Somehow, though, Master Skywalker had immediately seen through the deception. He had realized Brakiss's true identity. But unlike previous clumsy and unpracticed spies who had come to Yavin 4 with the same mission, Brakiss had not been expelled outright. Skywalker had shown little patience for those others—but apparently he had seen real potential in Brakiss.

Master Skywalker had begun working on him, openly teaching him those things he most needed to learn. Brakiss did have a great talent with the Force, and Master Skywalker had shown him how to use it. But Skywalker had repeatedly tried to contaminate Brakiss with the light side, with the platitudes and peaceful ways of the New Republic. Brakiss shuddered at the thought.

Finally, in a private and supremely important test, Master Skywalker had taken Brakiss on a mental journey within himself—not allowing him to look outward through the rivers of the Force, but turning the dark student inside to see his own heart, so he could observe the truth about what he himself was made of.

Brakiss had opened a trapdoor and fallen into a pit filled with his self-deception and the potential cruelties that the Empire could force him to carry out. Master Skywalker stood beside him, forcing him to look—and keep looking—even as Brakiss scrambled to escape from himself, not wanting to face the lies of his own existence.

But the Imperial conditioning ran too deep. His mind was too far lost in service to the Empire, and Brakiss had nearly gone insane from that ordeal. He had run from Master Skywalker, taking his ship and fleeing into the depths of space.

He had remained alone for a long time before finally returning to the embrace of the Second Imperium, where he put his expertise to work . . . just as it had been planned from the beginning.

Brakiss was handsome, perfectly formed, not at all corrupted as the Emperor had appeared in his last days, when the dark side had devoured him from within. Brakiss tried to deny that corruption—to comfort himself with his outer appearance—but he could not escape the ugliness in the darkness of his heart.

He knew his place in the Empire would be reborn, and he had learned to be content with that service. His greatest triumph was his Shadow Academy, where he could oversee the new Dark Jedi being trained: dozens of students, some with little or no talent at all, but others with the potential for true greatness, like Darth Vader himself.

Of course, the new Imperial leader also recognized the danger in creating such a powerful group of Dark Jedi. Knights who had fallen to the dark side were bound to have ambitions of their own, tempted by the power they themselves controlled. It was Brakiss's job to keep them in line.

But the great leader had his own protective measures. The entire Shadow Academy was filled with self-destructive devices: hundreds, if not thousands, of chain-reaction explosives. If Brakiss did not succeed in creating his troop of Dark Jedi, or if the new trainees somehow staged a revolt against the Second Imperium, the Imperial leader would trigger the station's self-destruct sequences. Brakiss and all the Dark Jedi would be destroyed in a flash.

A hostage to darkness, Brakiss was never allowed to leave the Shadow Academy. By order of the great leader, he would remain there, confined, until he and all his trainees had proven themselves.

Brakiss found that sitting on a huge bomb made it difficult to concentrate. But he had great confidence in his own abilities and in Tamith Kai's. Without that confidence he could never have become a Jedi in the first place—and he would never have dared to touch the teachings of the dark side. But he *had* learned those ways, and he had grown strong.

He would turn these new students. He was sure he could do it.

Brakiss smiled as he finished the report encapsulating his plans. The lanky Wookiee's anger was something to take advantage of, and Tamith Kai was the best at that. The new Nightsister was a born tormentor, and she carried out her duties extremely well. Brakiss would let her train Lowbacca.

He, on the other hand, would work with the twins, the grandchildren of Darth Vader. They were too calm, too well trained, and resisted in subtle ways that would prove far more difficult to deal with.

For them, he had other methods. First, he had to find out what Jacen and Jaina *really wanted*—and he would give it to them.

From that point on, they would be his.

13

THE SHADOW ACADEMY'S training chamber stood large and empty, a yawning, vacant space walled off on all sides. The doors sealed behind Jacen, imprisoning him with Brakiss, leaving him to face whatever the teacher had in store. The walls were a flat gray, studded with a grid of computer sensors. Jacen saw no controls, no way out.

He looked up at the beautiful man, who stood in silvery robes watching Jacen with a calm, patient smile.

Brakiss reached into his shimmering robes and withdrew a black cylinder about half the length of Jacen's forearm. It had three power buttons and a series of widely spaced grooves for fingerholds.

A lightsaber.

"You will need this for today's training," Brakiss said, broadening his smile. "Take it. It's yours."

Jacen's eyes widened. His hand reached forward, but he drew back, trying to hide his eager-

ness. "What do I have to do for it?" he asked
warily.

"Nothing," Brakiss answered. "Just *use* it, that's
all."

Jacen swallowed and did not meet Brakiss's
eyes, afraid to show how he longed to have his
own lightsaber. But he didn't want to have it in
this place, under these circumstances. "Hey, I'm
not supposed to," he said. "I haven't completed
my training. Master Skywalker and I had this
discussion just a few days ago."

"Nonsense," Brakiss said. "Master Skywalker is
holding you back unnecessarily. You already know
how to use one of these. Go ahead."

Brakiss extended the lightsaber handle to
Jacen, moving it closer, tantalizing him. "Here at
the Shadow Academy we feel that lightsaber skills
are among the *first* talents a Jedi should develop,
because strong, able warriors are always needed.
If a Jedi Knight is not ready to fight for a cause,
then what good is he?"

Brakiss pressed the lightsaber into Jacen's hands,
and Jacen instinctively curled his fingers around
it. The weapon felt at the same time heavy
with responsibility and light with power. The finger
grooves were widely spaced for his young hand, but
he would grow accustomed to it.

Jacen touched the power button, and with a
snap-hiss a sapphire beam crackled out, indigo at
the core but electric blue on the fringes. He
flicked the blade from side to side, and the molten

energy sliced through the air, trailing a faint smell of ozone. He slashed back again.

Brakiss folded his hands together. "Good," he said.

Jacen whirled and held the lightsaber up. "Hey, what's to stop me from just cutting you down right here, Brakiss? You're evil. You've kidnapped us. You're training enemies of the New Republic."

Brakiss laughed—not a mocking laugh, but simply an expression of wry amusement. "You won't kill me, young Jedi," he said. "You would not cut down an unarmed opponent. Cold-blooded murder is not part of the training Master Skywalker gives his young trainees . . . unless he has changed his curriculum since I left Yavin 4?"

Brakiss's alabaster-smooth face seemed exquisitely serene, but he raised his pale eyebrows. "Of course if you do let loose your anger," he said, "and slice me in half, you will have taken a significant first step down the dark path. Even though I won't be here to see the benefits, the Empire will no doubt use your abilities to great advantage."

"That's enough," Jacen said, switching off the lightsaber.

"You're right," Brakiss agreed. "No more talk. This is a training center."

"What are you going to do to me?" Jacen said, holding up the lightsaber handle, alert and ready to switch it on again.

"Just practice, my dear boy," Brakiss said, easing toward the door. "This room can project holo-remotes, imaginary enemies for you to fight, to help you hone your skill with your new weapon. Your lightsaber."

"If they're just holo-remotes, why should I fight at all?" Jacen said defiantly. "Why should I cooperate?"

Brakiss crossed his arms over his chest. "I'm inclined to ask you to indulge me, but I doubt you would do that—at least not yet. So let us put it another way." His voice took on a sudden hard edge, as sharp as razor crystal. "The holo-remotes will be monster warriors. But how do you know I won't slip in an actual creature to fight against you? You would never know the difference, the holo-remotes are so realistic. And if you stand there and refuse to fight, a real enemy might just remove your head from your shoulders.

"Of course, I probably won't do that in the first session. Probably not. Or maybe I will, to show you I'm sincere. You'll be here a long time training in the dark side. You never know when I might lose patience with you."

Brakiss stepped out of the training chamber, and the metal doors shut behind him with a clang.

Alone in the dimly lit chamber with its flat gray walls, Jacen waited, tense. Except for his breathing and his heartbeat, the room was completely silent, as if it swallowed all noise. He shifted, felt the hard Corusca gem still hidden in his boot. He took comfort in the fact that the Imperials had not found it and taken it away from him, but he didn't know how it could help him now.

Jacen turned the lightsaber handle in his hands, trying to decide what he should do. Intellectually, he was certain Brakiss was bluffing, that the man would never send in a real murderous monster. But a part of Jacen's heart wasn't so sure, and the slight twinge of doubt made him uneasy.

Then the air shimmered. Jacen heard a grinding sound and whirled to look behind him. A door he had not noticed before crawled open to reveal a shadowy dungeon from which something large and shambling scraped forward, dragging sharp claws along the floor.

Jacen's hobby back at home had been studying strange and unusual animals and plants. He had pored over the records of known alien races, memorizing them all—but still it took him a few moments to recognize the hideous monster that was now emerging from its cell.

It was an Abyssin, a one-eyed monster with greenish-tan skin, broad shoulders, and long, powerful arms that hung near the ground and ended in claws that could shred trees.

The cyclopean creature plodded out of its cell, growled, and looked around with its one eye. The Abyssin seemed to be in pain, and the only thing it saw—and therefore its only target—was young Jacen, armed with his lightsaber.

The Abyssin roared, but Jacen stood firm. He held up his free hand, palm outward, trying to use the soothing Force techniques that had proven so successful when he'd tamed new animals as his pets.

"Calm down," he said. "Calm down, I don't want to hurt you. I'm not with these people."

But the Abyssin didn't want to be calmed, and stalked forward, swinging its long arms like clawed pendulums. Of course, Jacen realized, if the monster was really just a hologram, then his Jedi techniques would be irrelevant.

The Abyssin pulled out a long, wicked club that had been strapped against its back. The club looked like a gnarled branch with spikes on one end, with a far longer reach than the lightsaber's. The one-eyed monster could pound Jacen and never be touched by the Jedi blade.

"Blaster bolts!" Jacen muttered under his breath. He flicked on the lightsaber, feeling the power of the energy blade that pulsed in front of him with a blinding blue glow.

The Abyssin blinked its single large eye, then charged forward, its fang-filled mouth wide open. The creature swung its spiked club like a battering ram.

Jacen slashed in front of himself with the lightsaber defensively, instinctively. The glowing blade sliced off the tip of the club as easily as if it were a piece of soft cheese. The spiked end clanged on the metal floor.

The monster looked at the smoking end of its club for just a second, then howled and charged again. Jacen was ready this time—his heart pounding, adrenaline flowing, attuned to the Force and focused on his enemy.

The Abyssin hammered down with the club, too close for Jacen to strike with the lightsaber. He dodged to the side, and the creature swung again, this time with a raking handful of claws.

Jacen made a dive for the floor and rolled, holding the lightsaber at arm's length to keep from harming himself with the deadly blade.

The Abyssin pounced on him, thrusting with the thick end of the club. But Jacen lay on his back and held the lightsaber up, twisting his wrists to slash the remainder of the club down to a smoldering stump in the monster's hands, then rolled sideways to dodge the heavy wood as it fell to the floor.

The Abyssin tossed away the useless stump and yowled again, then lunged to grab Jacen from the floor. But Jacen held the lightsaber in front of himself, pushing it forward like a spear. The glowing tip plunged into the descending monster's broad chest, scorching through until it disintegrated the Abyssin's heart.

With a loud and fading shriek of pain, the creature slumped and fell forward. Jacen winced, knowing he would be crushed by the brute—but in midair the cyclops flickered and dissolved into static, then nothingness, as the hologram projectors shut down.

Gasping and sweating, Jacen turned off the

lightsaber. The hissing energy beam was swallowed into the handle with a descending *thwoop*. He stood up and brushed himself off.

As the door opened again, Jacen whirled, ready to face another hideous enemy. But only Brakiss stood there, quietly applauding.

"Very good, my young Jedi," Brakiss said. "That wasn't so bad now, was it? You show great potential. All you need is the opportunity to practice."

14

LOWIE CROUCHED ATOP the sleeping platform in his own cell, back pressed to the corner, shaggy knees drawn up to his chest. He wallowed in abject misery and self-recrimination; occasionally he let out a groan.

How could he have been so stupid? He had let the riptide of Brakiss's teaching draw him further and further into his sea of anger until he had been immersed in it, swept away by its current.

Jacen had not given in. And seductive as Brakiss's teachings were—Lowie refused to think of him as *Master* Brakiss—Jaina had not succumbed to them either; she had merely stood up and spoken for what she believed.

A growl of self-reproach rumbled deep in his throat. He alone, who had always prided himself on his thoughtfulness—on his dedication to studying, to learning, to understanding—had allowed himself to be influenced by the poisonous teachings. He would have to be more careful in the future. Resist, block out the words.

If Jacen and Jaina could stay strong, then so could Lowie. Jaina had not given up. She said she had a plan, and he would need to be ready to do his part when the time came to escape. Lowie drew comfort from the thought of his friends' strength. He *could* resist giving in to his anger. He pounded a furry fist against the wall at his side and bellowed his defiance. He *would* resist.

As if in response to his challenge, the door slid open and two stormtroopers stepped in, followed by Tamith Kai. Lowie wrinkled his nose, noting something else that had entered his room uninvited: the unpleasant smell that hung about them, an odor of darkness. The stormtroopers each carried an activated stun wand, and Lowie guessed that they expected him to cause further trouble.

"You will stand," Tamith Kai said.

Lowie wondered whether he dared resist. A prod from one of the stormtroopers' stun wands answered the question for him.

Tamith Kai's violet gaze raked up and down Lowie for a moment, and then she blew out a short breath, as if about to start a difficult task that she had set herself.

"You are not yet skilled in the ways of the Force," she said, not unkindly, "yet you have the capacity for great anger." She nodded with approval. "This is your greatest strength. I will teach you now to draw upon that anger, to bring forth your full power in the Force. You will be surprised at how it will accelerate your learning."

She turned to the stormtroopers. "Remove his belt."

Lowie put a protective hand to the glossy braids that encircled his waist and crossed over his shoulder. He had risked his life to acquire these fibers from the syren plant as part of his rites of passage into Wookiee adulthood; then he had painstakingly woven them into a belt that symbolized his independence and self-reliance.

He opened his mouth to snarl an angry objection but stopped short, realizing that this was exactly the response Tamith Kai hoped for—to goad him into anger. He would not be so easily fooled this time. He stood, resolute and passive, while the stormtroopers removed the precious belt.

She motioned for him to precede her from the room. One of the stormtroopers administered an encouraging prod. Tamith Kai's smile mocked Lowie. "Yes, young Wookiee," she said, "your anger shall be your greatest strength."

They led him to a large, unfurnished chamber. Bright orange and red light glared down from unfiltered glowpanels set into the ceiling. The chilled air stank of metal and sweat. When the door slid shut with a hiss and a clang, Lowie looked around. He was completely alone.

Lowbacca stood waiting for what seemed like hours, alert, prepared for whatever Tamith Kai might use to provoke him. His golden eyes roved the blank walls with suspicion.

Nothing happened.

As he waited, the lights in the room seemed to glow brighter, the air to turn colder. Finally, he sat down with his back pressed to one wall, still wary, still watching.

Nothing.

After a long time, Lowie straightened up with a jerk, realizing that he had been about to doze off. He eyed the walls again, looking for any changes, and found himself wishing for even the annoying Em Teedee to keep him awake—and to keep him company.

Sound exploded in Lowie's head, high-pitched and excruciating, awakening him from a fitful sleep. Garish lights flashed overhead, blinding in their intensity. Lowie sprang to his feet.

Trying to focus his eyes, he looked around for the source of the siren and pressed his hands over his ears, groaning in pain. But he could not block out the sound that sliced into his brain as a laser would slice into soft wood.

Without warning, all sound ceased, leaving a vacuum of silence. The glowpanels stabilized, returning to their former level of brightness.

Tamith Kai's face appeared behind a broad transparisteel panel in the wall that Lowie had not noticed before. Still groggy from his interrupted sleep, Lowie threw himself against the panel in frustration. Tamith Kai's pleased chuckle sobered him instantly. "A fine start," she said.

Lowie backed into the center of the room and sat down, wrapping his long hairy arms around his legs, afraid to make any further response lest he lose his temper again.

Her taunting voice echoed through the empty chamber. "Oh, we are *far* from finished with our lesson, Wookiee. You will stand."

Lowie pressed his forehead to his knees, refusing to look at her, refusing to move.

"Ah," the voice continued, "perhaps it is for the best. The fire of your anger will burn brighter the more fuel I add."

The high-pitched sound drilled into his brain again, and flashing lights assaulted his eyes. Lowie concentrated, focused his mind inside himself. He mutely endured.

The lights and sound ceased as a heavy black object fell from an access hatch onto the floor beside him. Deep in concentration, Lowie didn't flinch, but he looked up to see what it was.

"This is a sonic generator," Tamith Kai's rich, deep voice announced. "It produces the lovely music you've been enjoying today." An undercurrent of cruel amusement rippled through her words. "It also contains the high-intensity strobe relay for the glowpanels. To complete your lesson for the day, all you need do is destroy the sonic generator."

Lowie looked at the boxy object: it measured less than a meter to a side, was made of a dull burnished metal with rounded edges and corners, and had no handholds whatsoever. He reached for it.

"Rest assured," Tamith Kai's voice came again, "even a full-grown Wookiee cannot lift it without using the Force."

Lowie tried to heft the object, found that she was correct. He closed his eyes and concentrated, drawing on the Force, and tried again. The generator hardly budged. Lowie shook his head in confusion. The weight itself, or the object's size, should not have mattered, he told himself. Perhaps, he reasoned, he was just too tired. Or perhaps Tamith Kai was using the Force to hold it down.

"Think, my young Jedi," Tamith Kai chided. "You cannot expect to lift the heaviest object with your weakest muscles."

Lights flashed again, and a dagger of sound pierced his ears. But only for a moment.

"Do not keep your anger pent up," Tamith Kai's voice continued as if there had been no interruption. "You must use it . . . release it. Only then can you set yourself free."

Lowie recognized what she was doing, and the knowledge gave him strength. He closed his eyes, drew a deep breath, and concentrated, prepared to resist the lights and sound.

But he was not prepared for what followed.

From all sides, jets of icy water exploded from the walls, buffeting him with bruising force. He was drenched and shivering, but still the high-pressure streams pummeled him, invaded him. The prying liquid forced itself up under his eyelids, inside his ears and mouth, and streamed down his body, chilling him to the bone.

As unexpectedly as it had begun, the watery attack ended. Shuddering convulsively from the cold, Lowie looked down to find himself ankle-deep in water that was barely warmer than glacial runoff. Anger welled up within him, but he suppressed it, let it flow out of him as the water had streamed down his body. He tried instead to shift the sonic generator again, but to no avail.

As if Lowie's effort had triggered it, the sonic generator began a fresh assault on his senses, strobing the glowpanels and flooding the room with high-pitched wailing until Lowie feared he would drown in it.

Instead, he concentrated on thoughts of his friends Jacen and Jaina. He would be strong.

When the generator paused, more fists of freezing water pounded him again from all sides.

How long these tortures alternated, Lowie could not say. After a time, it seemed his life had always been a litany of lights, sound, water, lights, sound, water . . .

And still he did not give in to his anger.

By the time Tamith Kai spoke to him again, he was curled into a tight, freezing ball of soggy misery, perched directly on the sonic generator in an effort to bring feeling back to his numb legs and feet.

"You have the power within you to end your ordeal," her voice said with mock pity. "Alas, young Jedi, fortitude is only admirable when it gains you something."

Lowie did not raise his head or acknowledge her words.

"You cannot help yourself in this way. You cannot help your friends. Your friends have already learned the truth of my words," she went on.

Lowie's head snapped up, and he voiced a growl of disbelief.

"Ah, but it is true," she said, a note of encouragement in her voice. "Would you like to see them?"

Before he could utter a bark of agreement, a pair of holographic images spun in the air before his eyes. One showed Jacen wielding a lightsaber, a look of fierce enjoyment lighting his young features. In the other Jaina used the Force to toss aside heavy objects, her head thrown back with a challenging grin.

Lowie reached toward the luminescent images with a yelp of stunned disbelief—and fell face-first into the icy water that covered the floor. He hauled himself back to his feet, and the sonic generator resumed its torturous whine.

From deep within him, horror mixed with rage and a sense of betrayal, fanning the embers that had smoldered for so long. Flames of anger sprang up inside him, warming him with their undeniable heat, rising higher and higher until they burst from his throat in a howl of fury.

And he knew no more.

Lowie woke to restful darkness back in his own cell. The room was warm, and he lay on his sleeping platform covered with a soft blanket. His muscles ached, but he felt well rested. He moved a hand to his waist and found that he was once again wearing his webbed belt.

The voice of Tamith Kai spoke next to him. Lowie was not surprised to find the tall, dark-haired Nightsister standing beside him. In the dim light of the cell's glowpanels he saw that she held an irregularly shaped metal object.

"You have done well, young Wookiee," she said.

Lowie gave a sad moan as the memory of what he had done flooded back to him.

"With your anger you succeeded beyond my highest expectations," Tamith Kai said, looking at him with obvious pride. "As a reward, I've brought you back your droid."

Lowie's mind faltered with confusion. Should he feel *proud* of what he had done? Should he be ashamed? He received Em Teedee from Tamith Kai's hands with relief and clipped the little droid to its accustomed place at his belt.

"You will make a fine Jedi," Tamith Kai said. She smiled conspiratorially. "After you unleashed your anger, we were unable even to repair the sonic generator, as we have every time before." And then she swept out of the room, leaving him to his thoughts.

Lowie stood and groaned as his muscles refused to cooperate, and he slumped back onto the sleeping platform.

"Well, if you ask my opinion," Em Teedee's thin voice piped up, "you caused a great deal of your own pain through your needless resistance."

Lowbacca growled a surprised reply.

"Who asked *me*?" Em Teedee said. "Well, I really don't know why you should be so upset. After all, you're here at the Shadow Academy to learn. Why, you're very fortunate that they've taken such an interest in you.

"The Imperials are very perceptive, you know. So perceptive, in fact, that they saw my own potential and have included me in their plans. I am most honored."

With an uncomfortable suspicion, Lowie barked a question.

"Wrong with me?" Em Teedee asked. "Why, nothing. Quite the contrary. As an expression of their complete confidence in me, Brakiss and Tamith Kai have had my programming enhanced. I feel much better now than I ever have. I am to be an integral part of your instruction here. You must realize that they have only your best interests at heart. The Empire is your friend."

Lowie made a thoughtful sound as if accepting Em Teedee's words—and reached down to switch the little droid off.

His head had suddenly become clear. Em Teedee's words had crystallized something in his mind. He might have given in, but he had not given up. And if he knew anything about Jacen and Jaina, the same was true for them—at least that's what he would have to hope.

15

IT WAS MIDAFTERNOON by the time Tenel Ka returned. She found Master Skywalker quietly contemplating in the small slave's quarters Augwynne Djo had offered him to keep him away from curious eyes during the meeting.

"I've spoken with the Council of Sisters," she said. Waves of afternoon heat rippled up the cliffside to the fortress of the Singing Mountain Clan, giving the air a flat, burnt smell. "They expect visitors to come at dusk. At that time all of our questions will be answered."

"Then we wait," Master Skywalker said, looking at her with his intense blue eyes. "It is one of the most difficult things to do—especially at such an urgent time, when we don't know what's happened to Jacen or Jaina or Lowbacca. But if waiting gets us answers where action would not . . . then waiting"—he smiled—"is the action we must choose."

• • •

Like a good guest, Tenel Ka busied herself with minor duties to help the Singing Mountain Clan as the hours crawled slowly by.

The sun swung toward the horizon and dusk. Low clouds in the otherwise clear air burned pink and orange, scattering leftover rays into the heated atmosphere. Clicking insects and scuttling lizards began to move about as their world cooled with evening, adding faint rustling noises to the day's silence.

On the lower tier of cliff dwellings, looking down upon the baked rocky plain, Tenel Ka and Master Skywalker watched the lengthening shadows cast by sunset across the desert. Compared with the bright reptilian hides Tenel Ka wore, Master Skywalker's brown robes seemed drab and nondescript—but she knew the strength and skill he harbored within himself.

Tenel Ka noticed something dark and large moving across the plain. She perked up and squinted her gray eyes, studying the creature as it came closer. Some large beast bearing a rider— no, two riders.

Master Skywalker nodded. "Yes, I see it. A rancor carrying two." Tenel Ka squinted again, then realized that Luke was enhancing his vision with the Force, sensing as well as seeing.

Others from the Singing Mountain Clan came to their open adobe windows and stood on the cliff balconies, gazing down in nervous anticipation.

The rancor plodded forward, slow but unstoppable. Tenel Ka could clearly see the hulking monstrosity, whose knobby, tan-gray body seemed nothing more than a vehicle loaded with ferocious fangs and claws. A tall, muscular woman rode in front; behind her sat a dark-haired young man with thick eyebrows, wearing a cloak of silver-shot black, just like the woman's.

"She's a Nightsister," said Tenel Ka. "I can feel it."

Master Skywalker nodded. "Yes, but this new breed seems well trained and even more dangerous. Something is happening here. I can feel we're on the right track."

"But—what is that . . . man doing with her?" Tenel Ka asked. "No ruler on Dathomir would treat a man as her equal."

"Well," Luke said, "perhaps things really *have* changed."

Below, the Nightsister rider pulled the enormous rancor to a halt. The clawed, lumpy-headed beast hissed and reared up, dragging its knobby knuckles across the baked hardpan. The Nightsister dismounted, and her black-robed companion slid down beside her. They stood between two towering bronze rocks that thrust up from the sands.

"Hear me, worthy people!" the woman called up the cliffs. Her shout echoed along the rocks, reflecting her words and making her voice seem louder and broader. Tenel Ka wondered how the dark woman could speak so forcefully. She felt the Nightsister's tug on her imagination even as she stood and listened.

"She's using a Force trick," Master Skywalker said, "pulling on your emotions, making you interested in what she's about to say."

Tenel Ka nodded. A cool breeze stirred up by the rapidly changing temperatures of evening whipped her red-gold hair about her face.

"Once again, we come to seek others interested in what we have to offer. Yes, we know that long ago evil Nightsisters ruled Dathomir with an iron hand and a cruel will. They were bad people—but that doesn't mean their training was completely wrong, that everything they knew about power is to be despised.

"I am Vonnda Ra, and this is my companion Vilas. Yes—a male. I can sense you are shocked and surprised, but you should not be. From other allies, we have learned that this power we call . . . *the Force* dwells in all things, male and female. Not only can the Sisters use it for their own benefit, but males—Brothers—can also wield such strength."

Many of the people in the cliff dwellings stirred.

"I sense your disbelief," Vonnda Ra said, "but I assure you it is true."

Tenel Ka whispered to Master Skywalker. "I have seen many things in the last few years," she said, "and I believe I know how other societies work—but I fear that some of the more conservative clans on Dathomir are not quite ready to accept such measures of equality."

Master Skywalker nodded, but pursed his lips gravely. "There's nothing in Jedi teachings that favors either male or female—or even human, for that matter. Your people have only been deceiving themselves."

Far below, Vonnda Ra stood beside her tamed rancor and shouted up. "Vilas, my best male student, will demonstrate for you one small thing he has learned, something that will amaze you."

Dark-haired Vilas removed his spangled black cloak and draped it on the patched whuffa-hide saddle across the rancor's back. He began to concentrate, standing off to himself in the flat, baked dirt between the stone columns, his arms at his side, hands clenched into fists.

Even from this far up the cliff, Tenel Ka could hear Vilas humming. Beneath their bushy brows, his eyes were squeezed shut. His black hair began to rise, flickering with static electricity. He rippled with a growing power.

Up in the purple sky, stars had just begun to shine through, bright white lights against the darkening backdrop of the almost-faded sunset. Clouds started to gather, faint wisps at first, like corded shadows across the sky that knotted and drew together. Tenel Ka stood back as the breeze picked up and became colder.

"We are always searching for new trainees," Vonnda Ra shouted up to the gathered crowd. The

Singing Mountain people clustered forward to their windows and balconies.

"If any of you would like to learn the ways of the Force, to do what Vilas and I can do—whether you be male or female, noble-born or slave—come join us. Our settlement is at the bottom of the Great Canyon, only three days' journey from here by foot.

"We cannot guarantee that we will choose you, but we will test your abilities. Any we find with the right kind of talent, we will adopt as our own. We will teach you to be an important part in the machine of the universe. Your future can be bright, if you are with us."

As Vonnda Ra finished, an ear-shattering peal of thunder drowned out her last words. Violent blue lightning danced in great forks that skittered across the sky.

Vilas had climbed one of the bronze rock pinnacles, scrambling up, light-footed, as if someone were drawing him up on cables. Now he stood on the flat weathered rock, arms raised. Static electricity swirled like a whirlpool around him as the gathering thunderstorm coalesced at his bidding.

More lightning flickered around the desert scape, striking solitary boulders on the flat plain and sending up showers of dust and sparks. The storm thickened, slashing at them with cold wind. Tenel Ka blinked back stinging tears as her hair thrashed around her.

Vilas stood atop his pinnacle of rock, commanding the storm. The clouds thickened, turning the sky black.

Tenel Ka looked down the cliff face and saw that beside the lone rancor, Vonnda Ra also held her hands outstretched, palms up, fingers spread, calling the storm. Lightning came down across the desert. The rancor snorted and reared, but did not run.

"Come to the Great Canyon," Vonnda Ra shouted above the screaming wind. "If you want to touch power such as this, come to the Great Canyon."

Vilas sprang down from the stone pinnacle and landed with ease on the windswept desert sands next to the rearing rancor. He and Vonnda Ra scrambled onto the patched saddle.

Vonnda Ra grabbed the creature's reins and yanked it about. The clawed monster loped off into the distance as the storm continued to rage around the cliffs.

Tenel Ka stared after, trying to keep her eyes on the dwindling silhouette of the monster and its two riders. "So now we know. . . ." she said. "What shall we do?"

Luke put his hand on her shoulder, and she could sense his confidence. "We go to this Great Canyon and offer ourselves as candidates," he said. "They *are* looking for new people to train. And now we're sure we're on the right track. Jacen, Jaina, and Lowbacca might be there already."

Tenel Ka bit her lip and nodded. "This is a fact."

16

JAINA LEFT THE lightsaber switched off and pushed it back toward Brakiss, but he wouldn't take it.

"I won't play your games," Jaina insisted.

"We do not *play* at the Shadow Academy," Brakiss said. "But we do practice. Important training for a Jedi."

"Fighting stupid holographic monsters? I won't do it anymore. I've done too much for you already. You may as well just take us home, because we'll never serve your Shadow Academy."

Brakiss spread his hands. "Ah, but you're getting so good with the lightsaber," he said, as if reasoning with a recalcitrant child. "Try it one more time. I'll give you a worthy opponent, someone a bit more challenging to fight."

"Why should I?" Jaina said. "I don't *owe* you anything. I want to see my brother. I want to see Lowie."

"You will see them soon enough."

"I won't fight unless you promise I can see them."

Brakiss sighed. "Very well. I promise to let you see each other again, during classes. But only"—he held up one finger—"if you agree not to cause more disturbances."

Jaina pressed her mouth into a grim line. For now, this was the best she could hope to accomplish. "Agreed."

Then Brakiss said, his tone disturbingly encouraging, "Think of it this way—the more training you undergo, the better chance you'll have if ever you fight against me. Consider it . . . training for your eventual escape, hmmm?"

She found the calm smile maddening on his smooth, handsome face.

"There will be another change in our session this morning. As you fight, you will be shrouded in a holographic disguise. It will not hinder your movements, but you may find it a bit distracting. You must learn to fight wearing this three-dimensional mask: for the good of the Empire, we may occasionally need to deploy our Dark Jedi in disguise."

Jaina held the lightsaber in front of her. "All right, I'll fight this one training session—then you have to let me see my brother and Lowie."

"That was our agreement," Brakiss answered. "I'll go arrange it now. Meanwhile, good luck." He slipped back out the doorway, and it sealed shut.

The flat gray walls flickered, and Jaina saw

shadows wrap themselves around her—not enough to blind her, just a blur. She realized it must be the holographic costume.

On the other side of the room an imaginary wooden door groaned open, and Jaina rolled her eyes. Just a corny illusion, as everything else had been. Jaina was not amused. Her only challenge was trying to figure out how the equipment on the station worked. Someday she would foil the Shadow Academy, bring its systems crashing down. For now, she would play along with Brakiss, and eventually she would find a way to turn the head teacher's schemes against him.

Her new opponent stepped out of the barred dungeon doorway—a tall, looming figure wrapped completely in black. The black plasteel mask echoed and hissed as Darth Vader breathed through his respirator.

Startled, she caught her breath, instinctively flicking on her lightsaber. Brakiss wasn't playing fair! This went beyond any of the other illusions he had sent against her before. Darth Vader had been killed before the twins were even born, but the Dark Lord of the Sith had been her grandfather; she knew all about him.

Vader's lightsaber was a deep pulsing red, like fresh blood, glowing with light from within. Jaina felt both anger and dismay rise within her, and she stepped forward to confront him. Her holographic costume swirled around her, but she didn't let it distract her.

Jaina hated the evil acts Darth Vader had performed during his alliance with the Emperor—but she also loved the *idea* of what her grandfather Anakin Skywalker could have been, the good man he had become in his last moments when he turned against the Emperor and ended his reign of terror.

Whether it was her own fear or something deeper, Jaina sensed a great uneasiness in the training chamber, a pulsating dread that slowed her movements.

Darth Vader took advantage of her shocked hesitation. He came toward her, scarlet lightsaber sizzling. His breathing echoed all around her. Vader slashed with the weapon, and Jaina countered with her own beam, producing a shower of sparks as the energy blades crossed and struck.

They struck again and again. Thrusting. Parrying. Attacking. Defending.

Jaina swung, trying to land a blow on Darth Vader's chest armor, but the Dark Lord brought his own beam up to crash against hers. She backed away as he attacked with greater strength, slashing, striking with his lightsaber. The shrieks of electrical discharge nearly deafened her. But as Jaina began to falter, she pretended Vader was Brakiss or Tamith Kai—the ones who had kidnapped her and brought all of them to this school of darkness—and was able to defend herself with renewed strength, this time pushing Vader back.

She struck blow after blow. The lightsabers

clashed, but Darth Vader seemed to draw strength from Jaina's fury. They fought on for a long time, neither gaining the upper hand. Jaina lost track of how many minutes or hours passed.

They stood with lightsabers crossed and electric arcs flying around them, pressing against each other, straining with all their might. But Vader could not defeat her, and she could not defeat him. They were equally matched.

She gritted her teeth and strained, her breathing heavy, her lungs burning cold. She gasped, but would not let up. Vader also did not stop.

"Enough!" Brakiss's voice came over the intercom.

The training room's holographic simulation faded, leaving her standing in the flat gray room, her lightsaber still crossed with her opponent's. Only now she could see who her adversary really was.

Jacen.

In the control room, looking down at the displayed images from the simulation chamber, Brakiss tapped his fingers together. With great pleasure, he watched the twins battle each other.

Wearing his dark Imperial uniform, Qorl stood beside him, observing the activity. The monitor showed none of the holographic disguises, just the twins fighting, battling to the death—and not even knowing it! Their lightsabers crossed and locked, neither twin overpowering the other.

Qorl remained silent for a long moment, fidgeting with restrained anxiety. Finally he said, "Isn't this dangerous, Brakiss? With one slip, those children could kill each other. You would lose two of your best trainees at the Shadow Academy."

"I doubt I'll lose them," Brakiss said, dismissing the thought with a wave. "But if one kills the other, then we will know which is the stronger fighter. That is the one we must concentrate our training on."

"But what a waste," Qorl said. "Why would you do this? What is the point?"

Brakiss turned to the old TIE pilot, allowing just a trace of anger to show on his perfect face. "The point is to obtain and develop the strongest fighters for the Empire. The most talented Dark Jedi."

"No matter what the cost?" Qorl said.

"Cost is of no consequence," Brakiss replied. "These young twins are simply tools to be used— as you are, as we *all* are."

Qorl frowned and watched the continuing battle. "Are you saying the twins are expendable?"

"They are ingredients . . . components to be installed in a great machine. If they do not meet our stringent testing requirements, they are no good to us.

"But perhaps you're right," Brakiss said, finally conceding. "They have both fought well and demonstrated their skills with the lightsaber. Now to make a real impact on them."

He turned on the comm. "Enough!" he said, and disabled the holographic disguise generator.

The twins cried out, then sprang apart, astonished to discover they'd been fighting each other.

After a few moments Brakiss switched off the intercom, not wanting to listen to the children's outraged cries anymore. He shrugged and smiled at Qorl. "I did promise to let her see her brother. I don't know why she should be so upset."

Qorl turned away and walked toward the exit, so Brakiss would not see the depth of his uncertainty. The harsh treatment of Jacen and Jaina disturbed him, affecting him against his wishes.

"Their training is coming along quite nicely," Brakiss said as Qorl reached the door. "I am pleased with their progress. They will become great Dark Jedi in our service."

Qorl made a noncommittal reply as he slipped out and closed the door behind him.

17

TENEL KA AND Luke rode astride a young rancor that had not yet been marked to show ownership by any particular clan.

The night air was warm and still heavy with moisture from the unnatural storm Vonnda Ra and her student Vilas had called up. Dathomir's two moons floated in and out of wispy clouds, shedding a diffuse pearly light on their path.

Tenel Ka sat in front of Luke on the whuffa-hide saddle, guiding the rancor steadily in the direction of the Great Canyon. She was a good rider, and she knew it. She had to admit that it felt good to demonstrate to Master Skywalker that she was an expert at something.

A light breeze rustled the leaves of the low bushes around them, so that when Luke leaned forward to whisper in her ear, Tenel Ka hardly heard him at first. "I had to kill a rancor once," he said. "It was a shame—they're such fine creatures."

"Even so," Tenel Ka answered, "they are dangerous to those who are not their friends."

Luke was silent for a while. "I've fought many battles," he said at last, "and yes, I have had to kill. But I've learned from the light side of the Force that it's better to do everything in my power first to . . . *turn* a situation—"

"But surely," Tenel Ka interrupted, "a Nightsister—or anyone else seduced by the dark side— would not hesitate to kill *you*."

"Exactly!" Luke's soft exclamation took her by surprise. "Now you begin to understand," he said. "Those who use the light side do not believe the same things as those who use the dark side. But we can only *demonstrate* our differences by acting on our beliefs. Otherwise . . . we're not so different after all."

"Ah. Aha," Tenel Ka said. "Just as *I* struggle to show that I am different from my grandmother on Hapes. . . ." Her voice trailed off. "Yes, I see now."

In spite of the darkness, their surefooted rancor picked its way steadily down the steep path that led to the floor of the Great Canyon. During their descent, they spotted a cluster of more than a dozen campfires, and knew that they had found the Nightsisters' encampment.

By the time they reached the canyon floor, both Luke and Tenel Ka were sore and aching and weary. The air was cool, with a light mist hovering close to the ground, and they were both glad of the warm cloaks that Augwynne had pressed on them during their rushed preparations for departure. She had given them each a change of clothes appropriate to their cover story, along with a bag of provisions. Then she had hugged Tenel Ka fiercely. "Daughter of my daughter's daughter," she said, "go in safety. The thoughts of the Singing Mountain Clan are with you." She turned to Luke. "And may the Force be with you."

Augwynne had released Tenel Ka and spoke again to her. "I am proud of what you do for your friends. You are a true warrior woman of our clan. Always remember our most sacred rule from the Book of Laws: 'Never concede to evil.'"

Now, as they drew closer to that evil, Tenel Ka shivered and pulled her cloak more tightly about her. She wondered if they would find Lowbacca, Jacen, and Jaina at the camp of the Nightsisters, or if that would only be an intermediate step in their search. Could the Nightsisters be training them in the dark ways of the Force? Tenel Ka let her eyes drift shut and cast about with her mind, but she sensed no trace of her three friends.

As if understanding the direction of her thoughts, Luke leaned forward again. "If we don't find them here, the Force will guide us. We are close . . . I feel it."

An ululating cry rang out from the canyon rocks above them. Tenel Ka started in surprise. "A scout sounding the alarm," she said, irritated with herself for having been caught off guard.

"Good," Luke replied. "Then they know we're here."

Tenel Ka hesitated at first, uncertain of whether it was safe to continue, and then urged the young rancor forward. She looked up at the sky, which had lightened from black to predawn grayness, reminding her again of how much time had passed since her friends had been captured.

Rounding the next bend in the trail, the rancor came to an abrupt stop. Tenel Ka looked at the path ahead of her and saw that their way was blocked by three full-grown rancors, each bearing a rider, dressed much as Vonnda Ra and Vilas had been earlier that evening.

The pressure of Luke's hand at her waist was a warning, but she already knew. Even in the dimness she could see that each of the riders held an Imperial blaster aimed directly at them.

Tenel Ka had been raised to take command, and though she rarely exercised that power, it did come naturally. She sat up straighter in the saddle and held one arm high. "Sisters and brothers of the Great Canyon Clan," she said, "we have heard your message as far away as the Misty Falls Clan and have traveled here to join you. We are not without skill in the Force, and we wish to learn your ways, to use *all* of the Force and to become strong."

• • •

Leaving the rancors at the well-provisioned stockade, Tenel Ka and Luke followed the guards toward the center of camp. She was surprised to see two Imperial AT-ST scout walkers clanking like mechanical birds around the perimeter on guard duty, near the penned rancors.

Passing between boldly colored tents made of water-repellent lizard hides, Tenel Ka noted roughly ten women and at least as many men going about their early-morning business in eerie silence, as if the warm ground mists swirling up to their knees muffled all sound. She saw no children at all in the encampment, heard no baby's cries, no sounds of young ones playing. In fact, she saw very few in the Great Canyon Clan who were even as young as she was.

Though she had known what to expect, it amazed Tenel Ka that men came and went here as freely as the women, apparently slaves to no one. She wondered if it really was possible on Dathomir that these men and women now thought of each other as equals.

At the center of camp, they came at last to an enormous patchwork pavilion that floated on the mist like a barbaric island made of furs and lizard hides sewn together. It was held up at the center and the corners by spears, three meters long and as thick around as Tenel Ka's wrists.

One of the Nightsisters raised a tent flap and motioned them inside. They entered, but the

Sister did not follow. The flap dropped shut behind them, sealing out the wraithlike mists and the morning light. Waiting for her eyes to adjust, Tenel Ka tried to sense her friends; she still found no trace, but the light touch of Master Skywalker's hand on her arm reassured her.

At the center of the tent a tiny pinpoint of light suddenly flared into a bright flame, and Tenel Ka saw that it came from an oil lamp fashioned out of the inverted skull of a mountain lizard. Beside the lamp, on a wide platform covered with furs and cushions made from the hides of a variety of wild beasts, an imposing woman reclined in a massive chair made from a stuffed rancor head. The woman beckoned them forward into the flickering circle of light.

Without so much as a greeting, Vonnda Ra asked, "What is your business here?"

Tenel Ka, who had recognized the dark-haired woman instantly, said, "I have come to join the Nightsisters, and I have brought my slave with me."

"What have you to offer us?" Vonnda Ra looked mildly interested, but not impressed. "Many come wishing to join us, but they are weak. Women seek us out because their powers are small or they have no status in their clans. Men come here because they have never had power, and our teachings offer them freedom—but they usually have even less to offer. What do you have?"

Vonnda Ra's hand reached out and pointed to

the lizard skull filled with burning oil. "Can you do this?" The lamp floated straight upward toward the peak of the tent, casting an ever-wider but dimmer circle of light, and then settled slowly back down onto the platform beside Vonnda Ra.

Tenel Ka nodded. "I have had some training." Deciding against using any theatrical gestures or words, she half-closed her eyes in concentration and grasped the lamp with her mind. She had never enjoyed showing off her skill with the Force, using it only when absolutely necessary, but this performance was not for herself. She would probably never see Jacen and Jaina and Lowbacca again if she could not show these Night-sisters her true potential.

She drew in a deep breath, let it out again. Without a sound the lamp glided off the platform and high into the air over their heads. Tenel Ka thought about the flame, feeding it with her mind and making it brighter, brighter, until its warm radiance reached even to the darkest corners of the pavilion. Then she sent the lamp sailing around the outer edges of the tent; it made the complete circle so quickly that she heard Vonnda Ra gasp with amazement. Through her half-closed eyes Tenel Ka watched the dark-haired woman sit up, one hand outstretched, palm up, as if to ask a question.

Tenel Ka brought the lamp in closer for another circle, and then another, smaller and closer to the central tent post, until at last it spun around the

center pole in a dizzy downward spiral, still
glowing brightly—all in a matter of a few seconds. Last, Tenel Ka brought the spinning lamp
lightly to rest in Vonnda Ra's outstretched hand.

The Nightsister gave a gleeful chuckle. "You are
welcome here, Sister," she said. "What is your
name?"

Tenel Ka threw her head back. "My name—*our
names*—no longer have any meaning for us. We
discarded them when we left our clan."

"Come here," Vonnda Ra ordered. When Tenel
Ka did as she was told, the Nightsister stood and
took the young girl's chin in her fingers and
looked deep into her eyes. "Yes," she said with a
satisfied nod. "You have much anger in you. Are
you willing to go elsewhere to learn? To a place of
instruction among the stars?"

Tenel Ka's heart leaped. Perhaps *this* was where
Jacen, Jaina, and Lowbacca had been taken. "Wherever your finest teachers are, that is where I wish to
go," she replied.

"But you must leave your slave behind. We will
have little use for him," Vonnda Ra said.

"No!"

Vonnda Ra sighed. "What if I were to tell you
that men rarely have any talent, and that we have
never trained one this old? He would only distract
you from what you must learn. There is little hope
of teaching him. If you knew all this, then what
would you say?"

"Then I would say . . . ," Tenel Ka replied,

leveling her best cool gray stare at Vonnda Ra, "that you are a fool."

Vonnda Ra's eyes went wide with surprise, but Tenel Ka did not stop. "This man has watched and learned the ways of the Force since before I was born. Not many—*not many who still live*—have seen his power. But I have seen it."

Vonnda Ra abruptly turned her skeptical gaze toward Luke. "If you can lift this," she said, pointing to her lizard-skull lamp, "*and* bring as much light to this tent as she did"—she nodded toward Tenel Ka—"then you shall accompany her."

The Nightsister looked at Luke and then back down at the lamp. When it did not move, a small contemptuous smile flickered at the corners of her mouth. Then something large and dark floated between them and blocked her view. The flame from the oil lamp brightened, and the massive rancor-head chair grinned at her, its lifeless eyes glowing with reflected light. Then the head lifted and glided around the perimeter of the tent like a shuttlecraft.

Tenel Ka could see Master Skywalker standing with arms crossed over his chest, one knee bent in an apparently relaxed posture, his head cocked to one side, smiling at Vonnda Ra as he sent the rancor head whizzing about the pavilion.

"Since you asked," he said, "I will give you light." Suddenly, in a blur of motion, the stuffed rancor head shot upward with the speed of blaster fire. It disappeared through the ceiling of the tent, leaving a gaping hole in its wake, through which the bright morning sunlight streamed.

Vonnda Ra looked more than a little nervous as she stepped forward and took Luke's chin in her hands. For more than a minute she gazed transfixed into his eyes. "Yes," she hissed at last. "Yes, you understand the dark side."

She backed away from him as if in awe, stared up at the rent in the ceiling of her pavilion, then looked back at Luke and Tenel Ka. "We expect an Imperial supply shuttle at dawn tomorrow," she said. "When it leaves this planet, the two of you must be on it."

18

JACEN, JAINA, AND Lowbacca were at first surprised and delighted that they would be together for the next exercise—but the grim expressions on Brakiss and Tamith Kai soon soured their pleasure. Obviously, Jacen thought, the two Shadow Academy instructors had something difficult and dangerous in mind.

"Because you must move forward in your training," Brakiss said, motioning outward to represent progress, "we have designed exercises to present greater and greater challenges for your abilities."

Lowie groaned in dismay.

"For this next test, the three of you must work *together*. Each trainee must learn to act in concert with others to assist our cause. There are times when we must be unified to provide appropriate service to the Second Imperium."

Em Teedee parroted from his place at Lowie's waist, "Oh, most certainly—appropriate service to the Empire."

Lowie growled at the translating droid to be quiet.

"You needn't take that tone with me! I am simply reinforcing the things you need to know," the reprogrammed Em Teedee replied, miffed

The three companions found themselves in a new room this time, smaller, more claustrophobic, with numerous round hatches built into the walls on every side.

Tamith Kai went to a control panel in one corner and tapped in a series of commands with her long-nailed fingers. Four of the metal hatches slid open, and spherical remotes floated out on repulsorfields.

The remotes were metal balls studded with tiny lasers. They reminded Jacen of the defensive satellites that had been unable to stop the Imperial blastboats from invading GemDiver Station. He felt uneasy, wondering if the floating drones would start firing at them.

"These remotes are your protection," Tamith Kai said. "That is, if the Wookiee can operate them correctly."

Lowie growled a question. "Oh, do be patient, Lowbacca," Em Teedee said. "I'm sure she'll explain everything in good time. She's quite good at this, you know."

Brakiss gestured to the remaining hatches on the wall. "These will open at random," he said, "and they will hurl objects at you."

Brakiss reached into the folds of his silvery robe

and withdrew a pair of polished wooden sticks, each about the length of Jacen's arm. He handed them to the twins.

"These are your only weapons: these sticks—and the Force. If the Force is your ally, you have a powerful weapon."

"We know that already," Jaina snapped.

"Good," Brakiss said, his intensely calm smile still in place. "Then you won't object to the other restrictions we place on you." From his sleeve he pulled out two long, black strips of cloth. "You'll be blindfolded. You must use the Force to detect the objects coming at you."

Jacen felt his heart sink.

"When the objects fly at you, you must either nudge them aside with the Force or strike them with the wooden sticks." He shrugged. "That is all. A simple enough game."

Tamith Kai took up the explanation. "The Wookiee will be in an observation chamber, working to protect you as well. He'll have full control of the computer to run these four remotes. They have powerful enough lasers to disintegrate any of the projectiles. Of course, if he misses, and the laser strikes you instead, he could cause serious injury."

"So"—Brakiss rubbed his hands together, a look of anticipation on his beautiful face—"you have your own weapons, and the Wookiee has the remotes. The three of you must work together to keep yourselves alive."

Jacen swallowed nervously. Jaina lifted her chin

and scowled at the two teachers. Lowie bristled, clenching and unclenching his hairy hands.

"Let me point out," Tamith Kai said, her voice thick and powerful, "that these are *not* holograms. These are real threats, and if one strikes you, you will feel real pain."

"Just what kind of objects are these, anyway?" Jacen asked. "What're you going to throw at us?"

"There will be three levels to your test," Brakiss answered. "During the first stage we will throw hard balls at you. They may sting, but will cause no permanent damage. In the second round, as the test speeds up, we will throw rocks, which could break bones and cause serious injury."

Tamith Kai's deep red lips wore a broad smile, as if she were savoring some pleasant thought. "The third round will involve *knives*."

Jaina sucked in a shaky breath.

"Glad you have such faith in our abilities," Jacen grumbled.

"I will be greatly disappointed if you are both killed," Brakiss told them, his expression earnest.

"Hey, so will we," Jacen said.

"I think *he'll* get over it before we will," Jaina added in a low voice.

Jacen shifted his weight on his feet and covered a wince as he stepped down on the hard Corusca gem in his boot. He had kept it hidden there, not knowing what else to do with it—but right now the last thing he wanted was to feel the sharp gemstone under his heel and be distracted. He wiggled his foot until the gem was tucked comfortably off to the side.

Brakiss snugged the blindfold over Jacen's eyes, and everything went black. "The Wookiee will do what he can to protect you."

Jacen gripped the hard stick in his hands and considered dealing the Dark Jedi teacher a good whack on the kneecaps, then claiming he had become disoriented by the blindfold and it was an accident. But he decided that such an act would only buy them trouble, and they needed their energy for other purposes.

"Good luck," Brakiss said, unseen, close to his ear.

Jacen didn't respond, and he heard Tamith Kai chuckle as they led Lowie out of the chamber. The Wookiee moaned, but Em Teedee's tinny voice snapped back, "Now, Lowbacca, complaining will do you very little good. You must learn to be brave and dedicated, as I am."

Jacen, standing in blackness with nothing to hold on to but his stick, heard the doors hiss shut behind them. "You ready for this, Jaina?" he asked.

"What kind of question is that?" she said.

The room remained silent around them. He could hear himself breathe, his heart pounding in his ears. He sensed Jaina beside him, heard the rustle of her clothes as she moved.

"Might be better if we stand back-to-back," she suggested, "cover each other as much as we can."

They pressed themselves shoulder-to-shoulder

and listened and waited. Soon they heard a hum of machinery, a quiet, grinding sound, as one of the metal portholes slid open. Jacen reached out with the Force to see through the blindfold, to detect where the projectile would come from.

Then, with a sudden *whump* of compressed air, one of the objects shot at them like a cannonball. Using his senses, Jacen whirled, swinging the stick like a bat. He tried to smack the ball out of the way, but it struck him on the shoulder. It was hard, and it stung.

"Ow!" he yelped. Then a second ball shot out. He heard the sizzle of the remotes firing, but then Jaina also cried out behind him—not so much in pain as in startled embarrassment.

He tried to visualize where the next missile would come from. The noises came faster now. He heard another metal porthole hissing open, another hard ball shooting toward him. He swung the wooden stick, and this time grazed it with the edge. He felt a surge of triumph, but realized that he had hit the ball more through blind luck than any skill with the Force.

Another hiss of a porthole, another ball, and another, coming from a different direction. Under Lowie's control, the remotes shot tiny blasts at the flying balls. Jacen heard an impact and thought perhaps Lowie had struck one of the targets. He hoped the lanky Wookiee wouldn't misfire.

Brakiss had instructed them to use anger to increase their control over the Force; as another ball hit Jacen in the ribs, the stinging impact did make him want to lash out in retaliation. But Jacen also remembered his uncle Luke's lessons: a Jedi knows the Force best when he is calm and passive, when he lets it flow *through* him rather than trying to twist it to his own purposes.

Jacen heard a loud crack of wood as his sister struck one of the hard balls. "Gotcha!" she cried.

As he let his mind open up, Jacen saw a small, bright blur through the blindfolded darkness; and he *knew* the next ball would come from that direction. He used the Force to nudge it out of the way, and the ball swung wide, smacking the wall instead. Then he saw another bright blur, then another, and another, as more projectiles came, faster and faster!

He used the Force. He swung the wooden stick, trying to keep up with the flying balls. He sensed that Jaina was also doing better, and that the laser bolts from Lowie's remotes seemed to be striking their targets more often. But with the sheer number of projectiles, Lowie had to miss occasionally.

Something hard and rough struck Jacen on the right arm just at the elbow, and the wave of blazing pain took his breath away. His arm went numb, and Jacen shifted the stick to his left hand, realizing that the test had reached its second stage—they were being bombarded with sharp stones.

•   •   •

In the observation chamber, Lowbacca worked frantically at his computer controls, guiding the four defensive drones. He fired their lasers and vaporized a few targets. But then the projectile launches picked up speed, and Lowie knew he didn't dare misfire—because if he struck one of the twins with a laser, it would do at least as much damage as one of the stones.

He missed another one, and a rock hit Jaina on the thigh. He saw her blindfolded face crumple in a wince of sudden agony. Jaina's knees buckled, and she nearly went down; but she managed to keep her balance somehow, swinging automatically with the stick and deflecting another stone that came straight at her head.

More sharp rocks hurtled toward the twins, launched with deadly speed. Lowie began shooting all the remotes at once—targeting, firing, targeting, firing. He had already slagged one of the portholes so it could no longer launch stones. But despite his best efforts, he missed again, and this time a rock struck Jacen in the side.

The twins were both hurt now, badly bruised and reeling, though they kept fighting as best they could. Lowie groaned a quiet apology and kept working at the computer controls.

Em Teedee spoke in a sharp, pestering voice. "Need I point out, Lowbacca, that the Empire will be quite disappointed if you don't perform to the best of your abilities in this test?"

Lowie didn't waste energy telling the translating

droid to be quiet. He worked the complex controls, calling up programming, reassigning parameters, hammering instructions with his left hand, controlling the remotes with his right hand, using everything he knew about computers. Lowie had a desperate plan—but his attempt absorbed part of his concentration. In his moment of distraction more and more of the hard rocks got through to pummel the Jedi twins. But Lowie had no choice, if he was to make his plan come off.

He sensed that in order to demonstrate their power, the teachers at the Shadow Academy were willing to risk hurting their students. As long as they were left with the strongest trainees, they didn't care if someone actually got killed during the exercises. Lowie's only hope was to bring it all down.

He glanced up, tossing ginger-colored fur out of his eyes, as the stones kept flying.

Jacen was on his knees now, dazedly swinging one-handed with the stick. His right arm hung limp at his side. Lowie saw that both of his friends were battered and bruised, and that still the rocks fired at them without mercy.

After a moment's pause, something changed—and long metal knives began flying out.

Lowie worked close to panic, but forced his concentration on the computer. It was his only hope. Jacen and Jaina's only hope.

The twins used their Force abilities to deflect the incoming blades into the walls, where they left long white scars on the metal. Another knife launched out. And another.

Frantically keying in more commands on the control terminal, Lowie let the floating remotes fall silent. He had one last idea. One last chance.

"Master Lowbacca," Em Teedee scolded, "just what do you think—"

Lowie punched in a command string that he hoped would bypass all other informational sequences, then executed it.

Five portholes opened at once, each ready to launch its deadly knife blade—

Suddenly, the entire training room shut down. The lights winked out. The porthole doors slammed shut. Everything went dark.

With a heavy groan of relief, Lowie slumped back in his chair, running a broad hand over the black streak of fur above his eyebrow. At last he had managed to crash the murderous testing routine.

"Oh, Lowbacca!" Em Teedee wailed. "Dear me, you've really botched everything up! Have you any idea how much trouble it will be to fix this mess?"

Lowie smiled, showing fangs, and purred in contentment.

Brakiss and Tamith Kai charged into the observation room. The Nightsister, her black cloak swirling around her like a storm cloud, was furious. Her violet eyes looked ready to shoot lightning bolts. "What have you done?" Tamith Kai demanded.

Brakiss raised his eyebrows, an expression of proud amusement on his face. "The Wookiee has done exactly what I told him to do," Brakiss said. "He defended his two friends. We didn't tell him he had to follow our rules. It seems he accomplished the objective admirably."

Tamith Kai's wine-dark lips formed a sour expression. "You *condone* this, Brakiss?" she said.

"It shows initiative," he said. "Learning to find innovative solutions is an important skill. Lowbacca here will be a fine addition to the defenders of the Empire."

Lowie roared at the insult.

"Oh, Lowbacca, I'm so proud of you!" Em Teedee said.

Stormtroopers brought out Jacen and Jaina, who stumbled as they walked, obviously hurt. Their clothes were ragged and torn. Scrapes and bruises covered their faces, arms, and legs. Blood oozed from a dozen minor cuts, and the twins blinked their brandy-brown eyes in the bright lights of the observation room.

Brakiss commended both of them for their efforts. "A very good test," he said. "You young Jedi Knights continue to impress me. Master Skywalker must be doing a good job selecting his candidates."

"Better candidates than *you'll* ever get," Jaina said, finding the strength to defy him despite her injuries.

"Indeed," Brakiss agreed. "That's why we decided to take some of those that he has already selected. You three were only the first we obtained from the Jedi academy. You've shown such potential that we are now ready to kidnap another group from Yavin 4 From there, we'll have all the Jedi students we could possibly use."

Lowie growled. Jacen and Jaina looked at each other aghast, then at their Wookiee friend. Even without using the Force, the three companions knew they all shared the same urgent thought.

They had to do something—and soon.

19

TENEL KA USED a Jedi relaxation technique, hoping to quell her nervousness before Vonnda Ra could pick up on it. Waiting beside her at the strip of packed dirt the Nightsisters used for a landing field, Luke looked serene, but Tenel Ka caught a trace of curiosity and excitement in him, as if he were embarking on a great adventure.

"There," said Vonnda Ra, stretching an arm toward the horizon where a glimmer of silver flickered. As Tenel Ka watched, the streamlined metallic shape grew rapidly larger.

"You are most fortunate," Vilas said, striding up behind them. Vonnda Ra sent him a questioning look, and he shrugged. "I felt *her* presence, and I could not help but come to greet her." He indicated the approaching craft. "One of our most accomplished young sisters, Garowyn herself, will escort you to your new place of training."

Tenel Ka guessed that Garowyn must also come from Dathomir, since the name was common enough here. Another Nightsister then. *How could so many Nightsisters have come together so quickly?* she wondered. It was not yet two decades since Luke and her parents had eradicated the old Nightsisters, yet here again was a growing enclave of both women *and* men who had been seduced by the dark side of the Force, lured by its promises of power. The Empire had been here as well, seeking new allies.

Tenel Ka gritted her teeth. Were her people truly so weak? Or was the temptation of great power, once tasted, too strong to resist? She renewed her resolve: She would *not* use the Force unless her own physical powers were inadequate for the situation. She didn't like easy solutions.

Tenel Ka stifled her feelings as a compact, shiny ship settled with effortless precision not far from where they stood. Although she knew it belonged to the Nightsisters—or to whomever had kidnapped Jacen and Jaina and Lowbacca—she marveled at its construction.

The ship was not large, probably built to carry a dozen people, but its lines were clean and smooth, almost inviting Tenel Ka to run her hand along its side. No carbon scoring stained the hull; its surface bore no pits, dents, or evidence of the meteorites commonly encountered in space and atmosphere. The overall design seemed vaguely Imperial, but Tenel Ka could not identify it as any type of craft she had ever seen before.

She heard a low whistle from Luke and a

murmured question, as if he were talking to himself. "Quantum armor?"

"Exactly," Vilas said, sounding pleased.

As an entry ramp extended from the sleek underbelly of the small craft, Vonnda Ra stepped forward to greet the woman who emerged, clasping both of her hands in welcome. When the woman stepped off the ramp, Tenel Ka saw that she was half a meter shorter than Vonnda Ra. Though petite, the newcomer was powerfully built. Long, light brown hair streaked with bronze fell to her waist, secured with just enough braids and thongs to keep it out of her way, as befitted a warrior woman of Dathomir.

Without further ado, the woman pilot broke away from Vonnda Ra and came to stand before Luke and Tenel Ka. Her hazel eyes assessed each of them critically. "You are new recruits?"

Before Tenel Ka could answer, Vilas broke in, as if desperately eager to talk to the pilot. "You'll find that they have remarkable potential, Captain Garowyn."

Tenel Ka heard tension and hope—and longing—in his voice. She wondered if Vilas could be secretly in love with Garowyn. Her features were refined, and her creamy-brown skin was set off to perfection by her tight-fitting red lizard-skin armor. The black knee-length cape she wore open at the front seemed to be her only outward concession to the fact that she was a Nightsister, and Tenel Ka guessed from the haughty set of her mouth and her shrewd eyes that Garowyn did not often make concessions.

"Vilas, busy yourself unloading the supplies," Garowyn said dismissively. "I will test these two myself." Vilas cringed and shuffled dispiritedly over to unload the ship, but Garowyn did not notice. She threw Luke and Tenel Ka a challenging look and directed a question at them. "What do you think of my ship, the *Shadow Chaser*?"

"It's beautiful. I've never seen anything like it," Luke replied softly.

"This is a fact," Tenel Ka said in a reverent voice.

"Yes, this is a fact," Garowyn said, apparently satisfied. "The *Shadow Chaser* is state-of-the-art. At the moment she's the only one of her kind." Then, seeming to forget that Vonnda Ra and Vilas even existed, she said, "I do not wish to waste time. Come aboard. When the hold is empty we will get under way."

With that, she turned smartly and headed for the ship. Luke and Tenel Ka followed.

As the *Shadow Chaser* accelerated into hyperspace and the twinkling lights in the forward viewscreen elongated into starlines, Tenel Ka watched Garowyn set her automatic controls and stand up from the pilot seat.

"Our journey will take two standard days," Garowyn said, moving past them and out of the cockpit. "I may as well acquaint you with my ship. No expense was spared for the *Shadow Chaser*."

She showed them the food- and waste-processing systems, the hyperdrive engines, the sleeping cubicles . . . but most of it was a blur to Tenel Ka.

"And these"—Garowyn pointed toward several hatches at the back of the cabin—"are the escape pods. Each is large enough to carry only one passenger, and is equipped with a homing beacon that broadcasts its location on a signature frequency that can only be decoded at the Shadow Academy, where you will learn your true potential."

With that, Garowyn resumed the tour, but Tenel Ka flashed an alarmed glance at Master Skywalker, who met her gaze with equal concern. Her mind whirled at the idea that another Jedi academy existed, an academy for learning the dark powers of the Force. A *Shadow Academy*.

Garowyn decided to test them thoroughly. She questioned Luke and Tenel Ka by turns about their familiarity with the Force. Luke was vague in his answers, but Garowyn—perhaps because she was from Dathomir and considered men to be of little importance—concentrated her efforts on finding out more about Tenel Ka.

When Garowyn asked what experience she had, Tenel Ka answered truthfully. "I have used the Force, and I believe that I am strong. However," she added, her voice growing hard, "I will not rely on the Force so much that I become weak. If there is anything I can do under my own power, I will not use the Force to do it."

Garowyn laughed at that, a harsh, cynical laugh that grated in Tenel Ka's ears. "We will change your mind without too much difficulty," she said. "Why else would you come to us for training?"

Tenel Ka considered this for a moment and phrased her reply carefully. "I have no greater desire than to learn the ways of the Force," she said at last.

Garowyn nodded, as if that closed the issue, and turned to Luke. "I refuse to conduct lightsaber drills aboard the *Shadow Chaser*, but we shall see soon enough how well you sense my intentions using the Force." She picked up a stun staff in each hand and tossed one of them to Luke. Luke stretched out his arm, fumbled slightly, but caught the staff before it touched the floor.

And so it went for most of the day.

Tenel Ka did the best she could at each stage of the testing, but she could see that Luke was holding back, not revealing the full extent of his power—she had observed Master Skywalker enough to know this.

After seeing him weaken or fail in several of the tests, however, a thread of worry began to weave through her mind. What if Master Skywalker had fallen ill? What if he couldn't use his powers? Or what if—it hurt to even think it—what if he had been wrong, after all? What if the dark side really *was* stronger? If so, she and Master Skywalker did not stand a chance of rescuing Jacen, Jaina, and Lowbacca.

Tenel Ka felt weak and drained by the time she had lifted her tenth object to satisfy Garowyn's sense of completeness. The titanium block wobbled and shook as she lowered it to the floor of the cabin.

Garowyn gave a derisive chuckle. "Your pride in self-sufficiency is your weakness." With that, she closed her hazel eyes, flung her head back, and stretched an arm out toward Tenel Ka.

Tenel Ka felt the hair on her scalp and her skin prickle as if lightning were about to strike. Her stomach churned, and she felt giddy and disoriented. She bent her legs to sit but found nothing to support her. She was floating a meter above the cabin floor. Tenel Ka stifled a gasp of outrage and attempted to use her mind to wrench herself free.

Garowyn's creamy-brown face was furrowed with cruel lines of deep concentration. "Yes," she said in a guttural, triumphant voice, "try to resist me. Use your anger."

Realizing that this was exactly what she *had* been doing, Tenel Ka went limp. As she did so, Garowyn lost her grip slightly, and Tenel Ka wobbled in midair. *So*, she mused, *the Nightsister is not as strong as she thinks she is.*

Then, pretending to struggle again to hide what she was doing, she removed the fibercord and grappling hook that she carried at her waist and looked around for an anchor point. She soon found something that would work perfectly: the wheel on an escape pod's pressure hatch.

Garowyn was still amusing herself with Tenel Ka's "struggles" when, with a practiced flick of her wrist, Tenel Ka flung out her line; the grappling hook caught securely on its intended target. Before the Nightsister could notice, Tenel Ka went completely limp again. When Garowyn's grasp wavered again, Tenel Ka jerked on the line and wrenched herself free, falling to the floor and landing painfully on her rear.

She looked up to see Garowyn's petite form towering over her. But instead of an angry rebuke, all she heard from the Nightsister was a short, sharp bark of amazed laughter.

Garowyn reached out a hand to help Tenel Ka up. "Your pride has served you this time, but it may be your downfall yet," she said.

"That is often true of pride," Luke said quietly, seeming to agree. His eyes assessed the Nightsister. "I believe I could do that."

Garowyn's lips twisted in a derisive smile. "What? You think you could fall on your— ?"

"No," Luke cut in. "I believe I could lift a person."

"So?" Garowyn chortled, as if rising to a challenge. "Do your best."

She crossed her arms over her chest, and her hazel eyes dared Luke to move her. Suddenly, her eyes grew wide with astonishment and confusion as her feet drifted off the floor and she rose a full meter and a half into the air.

"I can see that it is time to teach *you* the power of the dark side as well," she snapped haughtily. She closed her eyes and wrenched with all her might.

Tenel Ka sensed that Luke loosened his grip—but only partially. Garowyn still floated above the deck, but he allowed the force of her movement to turn her around and send her into a dizzying spin.

Then, never taking his eyes from the twirling Nightsister, Luke said, "Tenel Ka, if you would be so kind as to open that first escape pod."

She understood his intention immediately, and moved to do as he asked. Within moments they had the gyrating, disoriented Nightsister deposited and sealed within the pod. Tenel Ka's hand hovered above the automatic jettison switch. Luke nodded.

With great satisfaction, she triggered the launch. With a *whoosh* and a *thump*, the escape pod containing Garowyn shot out into deep space.

"Master Skywalker," Tenel Ka said, her face serious, "I believe I now understand how it might be possible, as you said, to . . . *turn* a situation."

Luke looked at her, blinked once in amazement, and laughed. "Tenel Ka," he said, "I believe you just made a joke. Jacen would be proud of you."

• • •

Later that day, when they dropped out of hyperspace and the autopilot alerted them that they were about to arrive at their destination, Luke and Tenel Ka sat in the cockpit looking vainly for a planet, a space station, *anything* on which they might land.

But they saw nothing.

Tenel Ka turned to Luke in confusion. "Could the autopilot have malfunctioned?" she asked. "Did we have the wrong coordinates?"

"No," he said, seeming calm and self-assured. "We must wait."

Then, as if a curtain had suddenly been drawn aside, they saw it: a space station. *A Shadow Academy*, Tenel Ka reminded herself. A spiked torus spinning in space, protected by exterior gun emplacements and crowned with several tall observation towers.

"It must have been cloaked," Luke said.

As they approached the Shadow Academy, docking-bay doors opened automatically, and Luke placed a reassuring hand on Tenel Ka's shoulder.

"The dark side is *not* stronger," he said.

Tenel Ka let out a long breath, and some of her tension drained away with it.

"This is a fact," she whispered.

20

DURING THE SHADOW Academy's sleep period, all students were locked in their individual chambers and told to rest and meditate, to recharge their energies for further strenuous exercises. It was just part of the Imperial rules, and most students followed them without question.

Jacen sat alone in his small cubicle, bruised and aching from the training ordeal. He dampened one of his socks and used it to soothe the many cuts and scrapes he had received from the sharp rocks and knives.

He and Jaina had requested simple pain relievers, but Tamith Kai had flatly refused, insisting that the aches would serve to toughen them up. Each twinge of pain was supposed to remind them of their failure to deflect a ball or stone. He used what he knew of the Force to dull the worst of the pain, but it still hurt.

Jacen sat cross-legged, trying furiously to figure out some escape before Brakiss launched another raid on Yavin 4 to grab more of Uncle Luke's trainees.

His sister Jaina was always best at making complicated plans. She understood how things worked, how pieces fit together. Jacen, on the other hand, who liked to live in the moment and enjoy what he was doing, was a bit more disorganized. He managed to get things done—but not always in the same order he had originally planned.

Maybe the most important step was to free Jaina and Lowie. After that, they could decide what to do next. Of course, the biggest question was *how* Jacen could free them all from their cells.

Then he remembered his Corusca gem.

Jacen nearly laughed out loud—why hadn't he thought of it before? He grabbed for his left boot, shook it, and was startled to hear nothing. Then he recalled he had put the stone in his other boot. He picked it up and dumped the precious jewel into his cupped hand. Smooth on one side, with sharp edges and facets on the other, the Corusca gem glowed with internal fire—trapped light from when it had formed deep in Yavin's core ages ago.

Lando Calrissian had said a Corusca gem could slice through transparisteel as easily as a laser through Sullustan jam. But then, Lando said a lot of things that couldn't entirely be believed. Jacen hoped this wasn't one of them.

Jacen held the jewel between his thumb and his first two fingers and went to the sealed door.

When Tamith Kai and her Imperial forces had stormed GemDiver Station, they had used a large machine fitted with industrial-grade Corusca gems to cut through the armored walls. Surely Jacen's little gem could cut through a thin wall plate. . . .

He ran his fingers along the smooth metal near where the door sealed. Jacen wished he understood machinery and electronics like his sister did, but he would do his best.

He didn't think that he could cut through the whole door using only the strength in his fingers, but Jacen knew where the control panel was. Perhaps he could peel back this side of the plate, get to the wires, and somehow trigger the door to open—though he hadn't the slightest idea how to do it. Still, he took the gem, found where the control box should be, and probed lightly with the Force. He sensed a power source here, tangled controls. This was it.

Jacen drew a generous rectangle with the gem, easily scratching a thin white line in the metal plate. *A good start*, he thought.

Pressing harder this time, Jacen retraced the rectangle, feeling the sharp edge of the gem gouging deeper into the metal. After his third effort, his fingers hurt, but he could see that he had made a substantial cut through the plate. His pulse raced, and excitement gave him new energy. He forgot all about his aches and pains.

One side cut through and bent inward. Jacen

gasped. *Almost there.* He sawed away at the long side of the rectangle. With a *clink*, the metal parted. The last two sides were easier, and he sliced through them quickly.

The metal rectangle slipped from Jacen's sore fingers and fell to the floor with a loud clatter. "Oh, blaster bolts!" he muttered. He was sure the other Shadow Academy students would wake up and that stormtroopers would come running.

But outside, the halls remained utterly silent, as if a cloth gag were bound around the station, muffling all sound. Everyone remained locked in their quarters. Only a few guards wandered the halls at night.

Jacen was safe for the time being. He peered into the hole he had cut, looking with dismay at the mass of wires and circuits that controlled the door. *Okay, what would Jaina do?* he wondered. He closed his eyes and let his mind open up, tracing the lines of the wires and circuits. Some ran to communications systems, or computer terminals mounted at regular intervals along the corridors, or lights, or thermostats. Some ran to alarms, and others . . . connected to the door mechanism!

Jacen took a steadying breath. *Now, what to do with those wires?* He probably needed to cross them, but in a particular way. There was nothing to do but try it.

With aching fingers, Jacen disconnected one of the wires in the cluster he had isolated and touched it to another, careful that the exposed, electrified ends didn't touch his bare skin. A little spark flashed, and the lights in his room flickered—but nothing else happened. He tried with the second wire and got no response at all.

Jacen hoped he wasn't setting off silent alarms in the guard stations. He sighed. What if none of this worked? Well, he reasoned, then he might have to slice directly through the door after all. He shook his stinging fingers, anticipating the pain. First, he decided, he would try the last set of wires.

As if sensing Jacen's impending despair, the door slid quietly open when he touched the wires together.

Jacen laughed aloud and looked out into the empty corridor. He glanced from side to side, but saw only a string of sealed, featureless doors. Glowpanels lit the metallic corridors at half illumination, conserving power during the academy's sleep period.

The door controls looked much easier from the outside, and he didn't think he would have any trouble freeing Jaina and Lowie—once he found them.

It proved less difficult than Jacen had feared. He had seen the corridors down which the guards usually led Jaina and Lowie, so he went in that direction, calling with his mind. *Jaina will be the easiest*, he thought. He tiptoed along, afraid that at any moment stormtroopers would come marching around the corner.

But the Shadow Academy remained silent and asleep.

Jaina, he thought. *Jaina!*

Jacen walked along, listening at each of the doors. He didn't want to cause too much of a disturbance, because the Dark Jedi students might sound an alarm if they noticed him.

At the seventh door he found her. Jacen sensed his sister, awake and excited, knowing he was out there. He worked the controls until her door slid open. Jaina burst out, hugging him. "I've been expecting you," she said.

"Used my Corusca gem," he explained, pointing toward his boot, where he had stashed the stone again.

Jaina nodded, as if she had known all along what her brother would do.

"We've got to find Lowie and free him, too," Jacen said.

"Of course," Jaina agreed. "We'll escape and warn Uncle Luke before Brakiss makes his raid on the Jedi academy."

"Right," Jacen said with a lopsided grin. "Uh, since I got us this far, I was hoping *you* could figure out the rest of the plan."

Jaina beamed at him as if he had paid her the highest compliment she could imagine. "Already have," she said. "What are we waiting for?"

They managed to find Lowie, who was excited

to see them, and Em Teedee, who was not. "I feel obligated to warn you that I simply must sound an alarm," the translating droid said. "My duty is to the Empire now and it's my responsibility—"

Jaina gave the little droid a rap with her knuckles. "If you make so much as a peep," she said, "we'll rewire your vocal circuits so that you talk backwards and they'll toss you in the scrap heap."

"You wouldn't!" Em Teedee said in a huff.

"Wanna bet?" Jaina asked in a dangerously sweet voice.

Jacen stood next to her and glared at the miniaturized translating droid. Lowie added his own threatening growl.

"Oh, all right, all right," Em Teedee said. "But I submit to this only under stringent protest. The Empire is, after all, our friend."

Jaina snorted. "No it isn't. Think we may need to arrange for a complete brain wipe when we get you back to Yavin 4."

"Oh, dear me," Em Teedee said.

Jaina looked around, casting her gaze from one end of the silent corridor to the other. She rubbed her hands together and bit her lower lip, considering options. "All right, this is the plan." She pointed to one of the corridor terminals.

"Lowie," she said, "can you use that computer to slice into the main station controls? I need you to drop the Shadow Academy's cloaking device and also seal all the doors so that no one gets out of their quarters. No sense inviting trouble for ourselves."

Lowie made a sound of optimistic agreement.

"Lowbacca, you aren't capable of accomplishing all of that," Em Teedee said, "and I'm certain you know it." Lowie growled at him.

"If we can all get to the shuttle bay," Jaina continued, "I think I can pilot one of the ships out of here. I've trained in simulators for various craft, and you know I was ready to fly that TIE fighter before Qorl took it."

Lowie tapped the keyboard of the computer terminal with his long hairy fingers. He hunched low to stare at the screen, which was not mounted for someone of Wookiee stature. Lowie called up the screens he needed, showing the status of the Shadow Academy's shuttle bay.

"Perfect," Jaina said. "A new ship just came in, still powered up and ready to go. We'll take that one, as soon as Lowie locks everyone in their rooms."

Lowbacca grunted in agreement and kept working, but he soon encountered an impenetrable wall of security passwords. He groaned in frustration.

"Well, there now, you see?" Em Teedee said. "I told you you couldn't do it by yourself."

Lowie growled, but Jaina brightened as an idea struck her. "He's right," she said. "But Em Teedee was reprogrammed by the Empire. Why not plug him into the main computer and let *him* get through for us?" She plucked the small translating droid from the clip at Lowbacca's waist and began opening Em Teedee's back access panel.

"I most certainly will not," Em Teedee said. "I simply couldn't. It would be disloyal to the Empire and completely inappropriate for me to—"

Lowie made a threatening sound, and Em Teedee fell silent.

Working rapidly, with nimble fingers, Jaina pulled wires, electrical leads, and input jacks from the droid's head case and plugged them into appropriate ports on the Shadow Academy's computer terminal.

"Oh, my," Em Teedee said. "Ah, this is much better. I can see so many things! I feel as if my brain is full to overflowing. A wealth of information awaits me—"

"The passwords, Em Teedee," Jaina said, reaching toward the recalcitrant droid.

"Oh, dear me, yes. Of course—the passwords!" Em Teedee said hastily. "But I remind you, I really shouldn't."

"Just do it," Jaina snapped.

"Ah, yes, here it is. But don't blame me if the whole lot of stormtroopers comes after you."

The screen winked, displaying the files Lowbacca had been trying to access. Jacen and Jaina sighed with relief, and Lowie made a pleased sound. His ginger-furred fingers were a blur as he descended rapidly through menu after menu, finally penetrating all the way into the station computer's main core.

With two swift commands Lowie shut down the Shadow Academy's cloaking device. Then, with a resounding *clunk* that echoed throughout the station, he closed and sealed every door except those the three of them would need to escape. He yowled in triumph.

Belatedly, the station alarms went off, screeching and grating with a harsh, piercing sound, unpleasant as only Imperial engineers could make it.

Lowie unplugged Em Teedee. "There, I tried to warn you," the silvery droid said. "But you wouldn't listen, would you?"

21

BRAKISS SAT CONTEMPLATING in his dim office, long after the other workers had retired for the night. He reveled in the dramatic images on his walls: galactic disasters in progress, the fury of the universe unleashed like a storm around him—with Brakiss as its calm center, able to touch those immense forces but not be affected by them.

Brakiss had just written up the plans for a swift attack on Yavin 4 so that he could steal more of Master Skywalker's Jedi students. He had sent the encoded message deep into the Core Systems to the great Imperial leader, who had immediately approved his plans. The leader was eager to get more ready-chosen Jedi students to train as dark warriors.

The assault would occur in the next few days, while Skywalker was no doubt still reeling from the loss of the twins and the Wookiee, perhaps even away from Yavin 4 looking for them. Tamith Kai would go along for the assault. She needed the outlet to vent her anger, to drain some of the rage she kept bottled within herself. That way she could be more effective.

Brakiss stood and looked at the blindingly bright image of the Denarii Nova, two suns pouring fire onto each other. Something was bothering him. He couldn't quite put his finger on it. The day had gone routinely. The three young Jedi Knights were doing even better than he'd expected. But still Brakiss had a bad feeling, a low-level uneasiness.

He walked slowly out of his chambers, his silvery robes flickering around him like candlelight. He let the door of his office remain open as he turned to scrutinize the empty corridor. Everything was quiet, just as it should have been.

Brakiss frowned, decided he must be imagining things, and turned back toward his office. But before he could get there, the door slammed shut of its own accord. Brakiss found himself trapped outside his office.

Up and down the corridor the few open doors also sealed themselves. He heard clicking sounds as locking mechanisms engaged all around the station.

Automatic alarms shrieked. Brakiss would not tolerate such an interruption in his routine. Someone would be punished for this. He held the storm inside himself and strode down the halls, intent on squashing the disturbance.

Jacen, Jaina, and Lowie rushed into the docking bay, tense and ready to fight their way out of the Shadow Academy.

A gleaming Imperial shuttle of unusual design sat in the middle of the brightly lit landing pad, still going through its shutdown procedures. Other TIE fighters and Skipray blastboats stood locked down and in various stages of maintenance. The alarms continued their deafening racket.

Jacen saw movement in the shuttle and frantically gestured for the others to duck down, just in time to see two figures emerge from the entry ramp. One of the figures crouched and drew a lightsaber.

"Uncle Luke!" Jaina cried, springing to her feet.

The second figure, a fierce-looking girl, whirled, ready to attack. Her braided red-gold hair swept like a burst of flame across her gray eyes.

"And Tenel Ka!" Jacen said. "Hey, am I glad to see you!"

Lowie bellowed a delighted welcome.

"Well, it certainly is a relief to see familiar faces in the midst of all this infernal racket," Em Teedee said.

"All right, kids," Luke Skywalker said, "we came to rescue you—but since you managed to get yourselves this far, I guess we're ready to go. Right now."

Jaina issued a brisk report. "We managed to shut down the cloaking device, Uncle Luke. Sealed most of the doors on the station. Won't be many people coming after us, but we should get out of here as soon as we can."

"How will we get the sealed space doors open

again?" Tenel Ka said, looking over her broad shoulders. "It will be difficult to open them without help from someone inside. Is this not a fact?"

Lowie answered her with an extended series of growls and snorts. He waved his lanky arms.

Em Teedee, his chrome back plate still rattling loose behind him, scolded, "No, you cannot do it yourself, Lowbacca. You're getting delusions of grandeur again. It was *I* who helped bring down the Shadow Academy's defenses and . . . oh— oh dear, what have I done?"

"Maybe I can help," Jaina said. "Let's get into the shuttle cockpit. We'll try it from there."

Up in the control center for the docking bay, Qorl stood amazed as the unexpected alarms continued.

He watched the three young Jedi Knights rush into the large room below. The *Shadow Chaser* had just returned from a supply run to Dathomir, and a sandy-haired man emerged with a tough-looking young lady. Qorl recognized her as one of the Jedi students who had worked on his crashed TIE fighter back in the jungle.

As soon as the alarms sounded, Qorl knew that Jacen, Jaina, and Lowbacca were somehow behind the disturbance. The other Dark Jedi students were pleased to have an opportunity to increase their powers and appreciated their training; but Qorl had been certain these three would cause trouble—especially since Brakiss and Tamith Kai seemed determined to injure or kill them.

Qorl had been gravely disturbed at the supposed duel to the death between the holographically disguised brother and sister. He also knew the dangerous testing routine with flying stones and knives had already been responsible for the deaths of half a dozen promising Shadow Academy trainees.

He didn't agree with Brakiss's tactics, but Qorl was just a pilot; no one listened to his point of view, no matter how certain he was. Yet Qorl served his Empire, and he had to do what he knew was right.

He opened the comm channel and gruffly reported. "Master Brakiss, Tamith Kai—anyone who can hear me. The prisoners are attempting to escape. They are currently in the main docking bay. I believe they intend to steal the *Shadow Chaser*. All of my defenses are down because of computer failure. If you can offer assistance, please come to the main docking bay immediately."

Tamith Kai's violet eyes snapped open, and she leaped from her hard, uncomfortable bunk at the first sound of alarm. She came instantly awake, her mind burning with demands to know what was going on. Someone was threatening the Shadow Academy.

The Nightsister threw on her black cloak, which swirled around her with glittering silvery lines, like the trails of stars during a launch into hyperspace. She reached the door to her quarters, but it would not open. She pounded on it, punched the override controls, but the locking mechanisms remained engaged.

"Let me out!" she snarled. Tamith Kai worked the controls once more, again with no success. Her rage built within her. Something was happening, something terrible—and she knew the three kidnapped trainees were behind it all! They had caused more trouble than they were worth. The Shadow Academy could find so many other willing trainees in all the worlds of the galaxy that regardless of the talent of these three, their potential for disaster was too great.

She would destroy them once and for all, and then the Shadow Academy could settle back into its smooth, regular routine, with Tamith Kai dominating and Brakiss running the details. Then she could be happy again.

Her fingers coiled, and a smoky black electricity curled between them. "Out!" she roared. "I must get out!" Tamith Kai slashed with both of her hands in an opening gesture as she cried her command.

With an explosion of power, the doors bent backward, folding down in a burst of smoke and sparks from the sheared-off wiring in the controls. Then using her bare hands, she tore one of the heavy metal plates completely out of its tracks and tossed it with a loud *clonngg!* onto the floor.

Tamith Kai stormed out, her eyes shimmering like violet lava.

Qorl's message came over the hall comm systems, and Tamith Kai did not let her anger slacken for an instant. *The docking bay.* She strode forward at high speed.

While Jacen, Jaina, and Lowie scrambled aboard the *Shadow Chaser*, Luke remained outside with Tenel Ka. He glanced back and shouted to the twins. "I need to know about this place. There's something familiar and . . . very wrong here."

"Yes," Jaina said. "Uncle Luke, the person running the Shadow Academy is—"

But Luke had become distracted—fascinated, really. He suddenly stood up straighter, his eyebrows drawing together. "Wait," he said. "I sense something. A presence I haven't felt in a long time."

He walked slowly across the bay and drew his lightsaber again, feeling a storm in the Force, a deadly conflict. As if in a trance, Luke strode toward one of the sealed red doors that led deeper into the academy station.

"Hey, Uncle Luke!" Jacen cried, but Luke held up a hand for the boy to wait.

They needed to escape soon—it was their only chance. They had to seize the moment. But Luke also had to *see*, had to know. Behind him, he heard the weapons systems of the *Shadow Chaser* powering up. The ship's external laser cannon turrets raised and locked into firing position.

When the red door slid open ahead of him, Luke Skywalker stood transfixed. He stared at the sculpture-handsome face of his former student.

"Brakiss!" he whispered in a voice that carried across the docking bay, even above the chaos of shrieking alarms.

Brakiss stood where he was with a faint smile. "Ah, Master Skywalker. So good of you to come, I thought I sensed you here on my station. Are you impressed at how well I have done for myself?"

Luke held his lightsaber out in front of him, but Brakiss remained outside in the corridor and did not step across the threshold.

"Oh, come now," Brakiss said with a dismissive wave, "if you intended to kill me, you should have done it when I was a weak trainee. You knew I was an Imperial agent even then."

"I wanted to give you the chance to save yourself," Luke said.

"Always the optimist," Brakiss replied in an airy tone.

Luke felt cold inside. He didn't want to fight Brakiss, especially not now. They had little time. But didn't he have to confront his former student somehow—resolve their conflict?

They had to go *now*. He needed to escape with the kids before the Shadow Academy managed to get its defenses back on-line again.

Brakiss held out his soft, empty hands. "Come and get me, Master Skywalker—or are you a coward? Would your precious light side allow you to attack an unarmed man?"

"The Force is my ally, Brakiss," Luke said. "And you have learned to use it to your own ends. You are never unarmed, any more than I am."

"All right, have it your way," Brakiss said. He brushed the fabric of his shimmering robe and made ready to step forward. His eyes blazed now, as if he held the fury of the universe within him, ready to unleash it from his fingertips.

Just then, an explosion of hot energy streaked past Luke's head from behind and melted the door controls. With a second blast from the *Shadow Chaser*'s laser cannon, the controls were completely fried. The heavy metal plates slammed back into place, sealing Brakiss and Luke apart from each other.

"Uncle Luke, come on!" Jaina yelled from the ship. "We have to go."

Luke shuddered with stunned relief, turned, and sprinted back toward the shuttle. He knew it wasn't over between him and Brakiss; but that would have to wait for another time.

Jaina and Lowie and Em Teedee linked into the *Shadow Chaser*'s computers, trying to open the station's huge space door from within. While they worked, Tenel Ka raced around the docking bay, sealing all of the red doorways, making sure that none would open. The ominous man in the silvery robes had stalled Luke, and they couldn't afford another skirmish like that. Tenel Ka had to seal the doors, just in case a contingent of stormtroopers made its way to the docking bay.

Luke climbed into the shuttle. Tenel Ka sealed another metal door, then ran to the last one. Just as her fingers touched the controls, though, the door slid open. A tall, dark woman loomed in front of Tenel Ka, crackling with angry energy and ready to attack.

Tenel Ka looked up and instantly knew what this person was. "A Nightsister!" she hissed.

The dark woman glared down at her with a similar flash of recognition. "And you are from Dathomir, girl! I claim you. You are a fitting replacement for the three I am about to destroy."

Tenel Ka stood in front of the Nightsister, her arms and legs spread like a barrier. "You will have to get through me first."

The dark woman laughed. "If you insist." She struck with the Force, an invisible blow that nearly knocked Tenel Ka sideways—but the young woman deflected it and stood strong, lips clamping together in determination.

The Nightsister drew herself taller in surprise, looking like a black bird of prey. "Ah, so you are already familiar with the Force. That will make it easier for me to train you, to turn you."

Tenel Ka remained tense and rigid, glaring at her opponent. "This is not a fact. And I will not let you harm my friends."

The Nightsister seemed to snap as her anger

came free of its delicate cage. "Then I won't hesitate to destroy you as well!" Her black robes rippled like a thunderstorm. Locking her violet gaze on Tenel Ka, she raised her clawed hands, fingers outspread, glossy dark hair crackling with static as her body charged with electrical power.

Tenel Ka stood directly in front of her, unflinching, as the dark Force built to a climax within the Nightsister.

Without warning, Tenel Ka lashed out with her foot, putting all of the strength of her muscular, athletic legs behind the kick. The sharp toe of her hard, scaled boot struck the Nightsister's unarmored kneecap. Tenel Ka distinctly heard the *crunch* of a breaking bone and tearing muscles as her blow struck home. The Nightsister shrieked and fell to the ground, writhing in agony.

Calm and self-satisfied, Tenel Ka stared down at her with cool gray eyes. "I never use the Force unless I have to," she said. "Sometimes old-fashioned methods are just as effective."

Leaving the Nightsister moaning on the floor, Tenel Ka jogged back toward the *Shadow Chaser*, where Luke was gesturing for her to hurry. She climbed aboard, and the ship doors sealed.

Alarms continued to sound, their clamor muffled inside the cockpit of the *Shadow Chaser*. Luke piloted the vehicle, raising it off the floor on its repulsorfields. Jaina and Lowie still worked desperately to open the heavy space doors.

With a loud *crrummp*, two sets of the red metal doors blasted open. Smoke from detonators curled out, and white-armored stormtroopers charged in, blasting at the shuttle.

"You'd better get that space door open," Luke said. "Soon."

Lowie yowled. "We're trying!" Jaina said, keying in a new command string, working even more furiously.

More stormtroopers came through. Blaster fire sprayed across the room. They could hear the splatter and boom of impacts. But the *Shadow Chaser's* armor held.

"We've got company," Luke said, staring at the sealed bay doors. "We're out of time."

"I can't get the—," Jaina began, and suddenly the heavy doors cracked open, spreading wide for the *Shadow Chaser*. The atmosphere-containment field shimmered in front of the star-strewn blackness, but now the shuttle could launch into open space.

"Well, what are we waiting for?" Jaina said, trying to cover her confusion.

"Let's go!" Luke shouted, and punched the accelerators.

Everyone grabbed the arms of their seats as the launch threw them back. The *Shadow Chaser* roared away from the Imperial station, leaving the huge, spiked structure uncloaked in space behind them.

Luke heaved a loud sigh of relief as he punched

the escape coordinates into the navicomputer. "Let's get back to Yavin 4," he said.

None of the young Jedi Knights objected, and they surged into hyperspace.

"Good work, Jaina and Lowie," Luke finally said. "I didn't think you'd ever get that docking-bay door open."

Lowbacca mumbled something unintelligible, and Jaina fidgeted. "Uh, Uncle Luke," she said, "I kind of hate to mention this, but—we *didn't* get the door open."

Luke shrugged, not wanting to quibble. "Well, we owe our thanks to whoever did it."

Qorl stood by the docking-bay controls, watching the *Shadow Chaser* disappear. The escape left absolute turmoil in its wake as the Shadow Academy scrambled to regroup. Qorl touched the space door controls, smiled faintly to himself, and then closed the doors. He would, of course, never tell Brakiss or Tamith Kai.

Brakiss came into the control room next to Qorl, exhausted and troubled. "Is our cloaking shield up yet? We must get it working. The Rebels will no doubt send attack fleets in search of us. We'll have to relocate. That's why this station was designed to be mobile."

Brakiss drummed his fingertips on one of the control panels. "I don't know what I'm going to say to our great Imperial leader. He can trigger this station's self-destruct sequence at any time, if he's displeased."

Qorl nodded grimly. "Perhaps he won't be quite that displeased . . . this time."

Brakiss looked at him. "We can only hope."

Tamith Kai limped into the control chamber, utterly outraged. Her eyes still glowed with violet fire, and her hands were set in clawed curves, as if she wanted to shred hull plates with her fingernails. "So they've escaped! You let them get away?"

Brakiss looked at her mildly. "I didn't *let* them do anything, Tamith Kai. I don't see what more we could have done. Our duty now is to get away and plan our next step—because you can be sure there will be another opportunity."

Qorl powered up the station engines, and they began moving the Shadow Academy to a new hiding place.

22

JACEN AND JAINA crowded together, pushing closer to the transmission area in the Jedi academy's Comm Center as the image of Han and Leia came into focus. The twins cried out their greetings.

Han Solo laughed in delight. "Looks like I didn't have to come after you kids in the *Falcon* after all!"

"And I didn't have to mobilize the whole New Republic to rescue you." Leia beamed. "We got Luke's report yesterday. The scouts I had out searching for you kids are already looking for the Shadow Academy." In the background, Chewbacca roared a message in the Wookiee language to Lowie, who responded in kind.

In the Comm Center, Luke Skywalker stood next to Artoo-Detoo, letting the excited young Jedi Knights talk. Jacen's words tumbled out in a rush. "Lando Calrissian says something like this can never happen again. He's already working with his assistant Lobot to come up with refinements to

GemDiver Station's security. I think he's even going to use Corusca gems somehow."

Luke spoke up. "Yes, but I doubt the Shadow Academy will come here again to look for new trainees. We know what Brakiss is up to now—I suspect he'll go somewhere else for potential new Dark Jedi."

"But we brought the Shadow Academy's best ship back with us," Jaina said. "And you should see the design. State-of-the-art. Not like any of the models in the manuals, Dad!"

Luke put a hand on her shoulder. "We need to offer it to the New Republic, Jaina. It isn't ours—"

Han interrupted. "Hey, Luke, you need us to send some mechanics over to check out the ship, try to figure out its design?"

Luke shrugged. "Go right ahead if you want, but I've got a skilled mechanic and an electronics specialist right here on Yavin 4, ready to start on the project right away—Jaina and Lowie."

Leia flashed a bright, warm smile. "All right, Luke. We'll send our engineers to study it, but you keep the ship there. Use it when you need to. You earned it rescuing Jacen, Jaina, and Lowie. Besides, you're an important part of the New Republic. We'll all feel better knowing you've got a safe, fast ship when you go running off across the galaxy—and don't tell me you've forgotten how to fly a fast ship!"

Luke gave an embarrassed chuckle. "No, I haven't forgotten—but I could still use the practice."

• • •

Jaina and Lowbacca sat in her quarters, tinkering with the holographic projector, making a coarse schematic of their new ship, the *Shadow Chaser*. The schematic was not as accurate as the one they had made of Lowie's T-23 skyhopper, but they would refine it as they learned more about the Imperial ship.

Lowie roared as the hologram lost its focus.

"Master Lowbacca says that he most fervently hopes a comet will crash into the vacation home of the designer of this subsystem," said Em Teedee from the clip on Lowie's belt.

Lowie growled down at the miniature translator droid. Em Teedee had been completely purged of his corrupted Imperial programming, and the irritating little droid was now back to his normal self.

"Well, how am *I* supposed to know that you don't wish me to translate Wookiee epithets?" the little droid said defensively. "Although you must admit, I certainly captured the feeling well. Why, think of all the idioms I have to parse during a single—"

Lowie switched Em Teedee off with a satisfied grunt.

Tenel Ka entered the Comm Center, feeling well rested. No nightmares had plagued her since her return to Yavin 4. She wondered what would happen now that a new order of Nightsisters had appeared on Dathomir, joining forces with the Empire, but at least they did not haunt her dreams.

Tenel Ka made contact with the Hapan Royal Household; she spoke to her parents, assured them that she was unharmed, and passed along greetings from the Singing Mountain Clan. Then, steeling herself for a set of imperious orders, she asked to speak with her grandmother, the Royal Matriarch.

When her grandmother's face appeared on the screen behind its customary half veil, her eyes carried a smile and something else Tenel Ka wasn't sure she could read—surprise?

"Thank you for remembering to call. My sources tell me I should be very proud of you," the Matriarch said, with what seemed to be genuine pleasure. "I'm sorry that my ambassador wasn't able to visit you. Now, I'm afraid the meeting will be delayed indefinitely. I was forced to send Yfra on an urgent errand to the Duros system."

Tenel Ka's mouth opened, but she could not think of a response.

"But you'll forgive a concerned grandmother if she tries to find a way to look out for her grand-daughter from a distance, won't you? One or two unobtrusive guards in a nearby system, perhaps? I think that might be the best thing for both of us."

The image of her grandmother leaned forward to turn off the communication link, but just as the connection broke the Matriarch whispered, "Besides, I have a feeling you weren't terribly disappointed to miss Ambassador Yfra."

"This," Tenel Ka muttered, "is a fact." And she realized it was the first time in years that she had agreed with her grandmother.

Jacen stood atop the Great Temple on Yavin 4, waiting for Master Skywalker. In the aftermath of the morning's rainstorm, reflected orange light from the giant planet pierced the gray clouds overhead and gilded their edges with a warm glow. The light breeze ruffled his hair and spattered him with an occasional raindrop.

As much as he dreaded the reprimand Uncle Luke was almost certain to deliver, Jacen was glad to be back on the jungle moon. In the day since their return from the Shadow Academy, the Jedi Master had already spoken privately with Jaina and with Lowie. Though he had no idea what Luke had said to either of them, both had been quiet and reserved afterward.

And now it was his turn.

Jacen sensed Master Skywalker's presence even without seeing him as Luke came to stand quietly next to him. For a long time, neither said a word, as if by mutual agreement. Gradually Jacen relaxed. He was ready for anything the Jedi Master had to say to him.

Almost anything.

"Take this," Luke said, pressing a metallic cylinder into Jacen's hands. "Show me what you learned."

Surprised, Jacen looked down at Luke's lightsaber. The weapon was solid and heavy, its handle warm as his own skin. He hefted it, studied it, ran a finger along the ridges of its grip up to the ignition stud. His eyes closed. In his mind, he could hear the hum of the lightsaber, feel its pulsing rhythm as the weapon sliced through the air. . . .

Jacen opened his eyes and squared his shoulders. "This is what I learned," he said, handing the lightsaber back to the Jedi Master without igniting it. "You were right: I'm not ready. The weapon of the Jedi is not to be taken up lightly."

"Even so, you learned to use it. Didn't Brakiss teach you?"

Jacen nodded. "I'm physically capable. I know how to fight an opponent with it—but I'm not sure I'm ready mentally. Maybe I'm not mature enough emotionally."

"You didn't enjoy the fighting as much as you had thought you would?" Luke raised his eyebrows.

"Yes. No. Well, yes—I learned some things. . . . I'm just not sure they were the *right* things. A lightsaber isn't just some impressive tool to dazzle and amaze your friends. It's such a big responsibility. One mistake could get an innocent person killed."

Luke nodded, his blue eyes twinkling with understanding. "It sometimes feels like too great a responsibility, even to me. But the Force guides us as we fight. Not simply how to defeat our enemies—but also to know when *not* to defeat them."

Their eyes locked. "Even if what our enemies teach or do is evil?" Jacen said.

Luke Skywalker's gaze did not waver. "No one is completely evil. Or completely good." He flashed a rueful smile. "At least nobody *I've* ever met."

"But Brakiss—" Jacen began.

"Brakiss passes the teachings of the dark side on to his students. You heard him teach. But a teacher is not always right. And because you thought for yourself, you knew not to believe him." Master Skywalker nodded approvingly.

Jacen thought this over. "Brakiss let me do what I wanted to do more than anything else: practice with a lightsaber. But I couldn't trust him. He was hoping to turn me to the dark side, to use me for the Empire. I *do* trust you, though. You were right about the lightsaber, and I'll wait until you think I'm ready."

Luke looked up toward the clouds, which were breaking up, letting more and more light through. "With the Shadow Academy out there, and the young Dark Jedi that Brakiss is training, I'm afraid that time will come all too soon."

An old friend could become a new enemy . . .

STAR WARS®
YOUNG JEDI KNIGHTS

The Lost Ones

During a break in training, Jacen and Jaina are reunited
with their old friend Zekk, an orphan living in the under-
ground mazes of their home planet of Coruscant. Young,
wild, and free, Zekk has never had a care in the world . . .
until now. He sees the changes in his friends. Jacen and
Jaina have learned so much, have grown in so many ways.
Compared to them, he is only a lost little boy.

However, a powerful being has seen his potential. Someone who knows about shame and jealousy—and how to
make use of them. Someone who knows that the dark side
of the Force is especially attractive when you've got
nothing to lose . . .

Turn the page for a special preview of the next book in the
STAR WARS: YOUNG JEDI KNIGHTS series:
The Lost Ones
Coming in December from Boulevard Books!

IN THE OPEN air Jaina waited next to Low-bacca, Tenel Ka, and Jacen as they stood in one of Coruscant's busy tourism information centers, a deck that jutted from the grandiose pyramid-shaped Palace. Dignitaries and sight-seers from across the galaxy came to the capital world to spend their credits visiting parks, museums, odd sculptures, and struc-tures erected by ancient alien artisans.

A boxy brochure droid floated along on its repulsorlifts, babbling in an enthusiastic me-chanical voice. It cheerfully listed the most wonderful sights to see, recommended eating establishments catering to various biochem-istries, and gave instructions on how to ar-range tours for all body types, atmosphere requirements, and languages.

Jaina fidgeted as she studied the bustling

209

crowd—white-robed ambassadors, busy droids, and exotic creatures leashed to other strange creatures. She couldn't tell which were the masters and which the pets.

"So where is he?" Jacen said, putting his hands on his hips. His hair was tousled and his face flushed as he scanned the crowd for a familiar face.

The four young Jedi Knights stood under a sculpture of a gargoyle that broadcast shuttle arrival times from a speaker mounted in its stone mouth. Gazing up at the cloud-frothed sky, Jaina watched the silvery shapes of shuttles descending from orbit. She tried to amuse herself by identifying the vehicle types as they passed, but all the while she wondered what had delayed their friend Zekk. She checked her chronometer again and saw he was only about two standard minutes late. She was just anxious to see him again.

Suddenly, a figure dropped directly in front of her from the gargoyle statue overhead—a wiry youth with shoulder-length hair one shade lighter than black. He wore a broad grin on his narrow face, and his sparkling green eyes, wide with delight, showed a darker corona surrounding the emerald irises. "Hi, guys!"

Jaina gasped, but Tenel Ka reacted with dizzying speed. In the fraction of a second following Zekk's landing, the warrior girl whipped out her fibercord rope and snapped a lasso around him, pulling the strand tight.

"Hey!" the boy cried. "Is this the way Jedi Knights greet people?"

Jacen laughed and slapped Tenel Ka on the back. "Good one!" he said. "Tenel Ka, meet our friend Zekk."

Tenel Ka blinked once. "It is a pleasure."

The wiry boy struggled against the restraining cords. "Likewise," he said sheepishly. "Now, if you wouldn't mind untying me? . . ."

Tenel Ka flicked her wrist to release the fibercord.

While Zekk indignantly brushed himself off, Jaina introduced their Wookiee friend Lowbacca. Jaina grinned as she watched Zekk. Though the older boy had a slight build, he was tough as blaster-proof armor. Under the smudges of dirt and grime on his cheeks, she thought, he was probably rather nice-looking—but then, *she* wasn't one to talk about smudges on the face, was she?

Recovering himself, Zekk raised his eyebrows and flashed a roguish smile. "I've been waiting for you guys," he said. "We've got plenty of stuff to see and do . . . and I need your help to salvage something."

"Where are we headed?" Jacen asked.

Zekk grinned. "Someplace we're not supposed to go—of course."

Jaina laughed. "Well then, what are we waiting for?"

Jacen looked out at the sprawling city and thought of all the places he had yet to explore.

Coruscant had been the government world not only of the New Republic, but also of the Empire, and of the Old Republic before that. Skyscrapers covered virtually every open space, built higher and higher as the centuries passed and new governments moved in. The tallest buildings were kilometers high. Many had been destroyed during the bloody battles of the Rebellion and had recently been rebuilt by huge construction droids. Other parts of the planet-wide city remained a jumble of decay and wreckage, their abandoned lower levels and piled garbage forgotten over the years.

The buildings were so high that the gaps between them formed sheer canyons that vanished to a point in the dark depths where sunlight never penetrated. Crosswalks and pedestrian tubes linked the buildings, weaving them together into a giant maze. The lower forty or fifty floors were generally restricted from normal traffic; only refugees and daring big-game hunters in search of monstrous urban scavengers were willing to risk venturing into the shadowy underworld.

Like a native guide, Zekk led the four friends down connecting elevators, slide tubes, and rusty metal stairs, and across the catwalks from one building to another. Jacen followed, exhilarated. He wasn't sure he knew exactly where they were anymore, but he loved to explore new places, never knowing what sort of interesting plants or creatures he might find.

The skyscraper walls rose like glass-and-metal cliff faces, with only a narrow wedge of daylight shining from above. As Zekk took the companions farther down, the buildings seemed broader, the walls rougher. Mushy blobs of fungus grew from cracks in the massive construction blocks; fringed lichens, some glowing with phosphorescent light, caked the walls. Lowbacca looked decidedly uneasy, and Jacen remembered that the lanky Wookiee had grown up on Kashyyyk, where the deep

forest underworld was an extremely dangerous place.

High overhead Jacen could hear the cries
of sleek winged creatures—predatory hawk-
bats that lived in the city on Coruscant. The
breeze picked up, carrying with it heavy,
warm scents of rotting garbage from far
below. His stomach grew queasy, but he
pressed on. Zekk didn't seem to notice. Tenel
Ka, Lowie, and Jaina hurried behind them.

They proceeded across a roofed-in walkway where many of the transparisteel ceiling
panels had been smashed out, leaving only a
wire reinforcement mesh that whistled in the
breezes. Jacen noted etched symbols along
the walls, all of them vaguely threatening.
Some reminded Jacen of curved knives and
fanged mouths, but the most common design
showed a sharp triangle surrounding a targeting cross. It looked to Jacen like the tip of
an arrow heading straight between his eyes.

"Hey, Zekk, what's that design?" He pointed
to the triangular symbol.

Frowning, Zekk glanced around them in all
directions and then whispered, "It means we
have to be very quiet down here and move as
fast as we can. We don't want to go into any
of these buildings."

"But why not?" Jacen piped up.

"The Lost Ones," Zekk said. "It's a gang. They live down here—kids who ran away from home or were abandoned by their parents because they were so much trouble. Nasty types, mostly."

"Let's hope they stay lost," Jaina said.

Zekk glanced up, his forehead creased with troubled thoughts. "The Lost Ones might even be looking at us right now, but they've never managed to catch me yet," he said. "It's like a game between us."

"How have you managed to get away from them all the time?" Jaina whispered.

"I'm just good at it. Like I'm a good scavenger," Zekk answered, sounding cocky. "I may not be in training as a Jedi Knight, but I make do with what skills I've got. Just streetwise, I guess. But," he continued, "even though I have kind of an . . . understanding with them, I'd rather not push it. Especially not while I'm with the twin children of the Chief of State."

"This is a fact," Tenel Ka said grimly. She kept her hands close to her utility belt in case she needed to draw a weapon.

Zekk quickly ushered them through dilapidated corridors that were heavily decorated with the gang symbols. Jacen saw signs of recent habitation, wrappers from prepackaged food, bright metallic spots where salvaged equipment had been torn away from its housings.

At last they moved on to deeper levels. Zekk confessed even he had not fully explored this far down. They all breathed more easily. "I think it's a shortcut," he said. "I need your help so I can recover something very valuable." He raised his dark eyebrows. "I think you'll like it—particularly you, Jacen."

Zekk made his living by scavenging: salvaging lost equipment, removing scraps of precious metal from abandoned dwellings. He found lost treasures to sell to inventors, spare parts to repair obsolete machines, trinkets that could be turned into souvenirs. He seemed to have a real skill for finding items that other scavengers had missed over the centuries, somehow knowing where to look, sometimes in the unlikeliest of places.

They descended an outer staircase, slick with damp moss from moisture trickling down the walls. Jacen had to squint just to see the steps. As they turned the corner of the building, Zekk stopped in surprise. In the dim light reflected from far above, Jacen could see a strange jumble protruding from the side of the building—smashed construction bricks, naked durasteel girders . . . and a crashed transport shuttle. From the drooping algae and fungus growing on its outer hull, the damaged shuttle looked to have been there a long time.

"Wow!" Zekk said. "I didn't even know this was here." He hurried forward, edging his way along the damaged walkway. "I don't believe it. The salvage hasn't even been picked over. See—I'm lucky again!"

"That's an Old Republic craft," Jaina said. "At least seventy years old. They haven't used those in . . . I can't even remember. What a find!"

Tenel Ka and Lowie held the creaking ship steady as Zekk scrambled inside to look around. He poked into storage compartments, looking for valuables. "Plenty of components are still intact. Engine still looks good," he called. "Whoa, and here's the driver. I guess his parking permit ran out."

Jacen came up behind him to see a tattered skeleton strapped into the cockpit.

"Oh, do be careful," Em Teedee said from Lowbacca's waist. "Abandoned vehicles can be terribly dangerous—and you might get dirty as well."

"Was this what you wished to show us, Zekk?" Tenel Ka said.

The older boy stood, bumping his head on

a bent girder that ran along the shuttle's ceiling. "No, no, this is a new discovery. I'll have to spend a lot more time down here." He grinned. Engine grease smudged his face, and his hands were grimy from digging through compartments. "I can get this stuff later. I need your help for something different. Let's go."

Zekk scrambled out of the shuttle wreckage and grasped the rusted handrail on the rickety walkway. He looked around to get his bearings, making certain he wouldn't forget the location of this prize. The skull of the unlucky pilot stared out at them with empty eye sockets.

"Looks like you really do know this place like the back of your hand," Jacen commented as Zekk led them elsewhere.

"I've had plenty of practice," Zekk said. "*Some* of us don't take regular trips off planet and go to diplomatic functions all the time. I have to amuse myself with what I can find."

It was midmorning by the time they reached Zekk's destination. The dark-haired boy rubbed his hands together in anticipation, and pointed far below. "Down there— can you see it?"

Jacen looked down, *down* over a ledge to

see a rusted construction crawler latched to a wall about ten meters away . . . completely out of reach. The construction crawler was a cranelike mechanical apparatus that had once ridden tracks along the side of the building, scouring the walls clean, effecting repairs, applying duracrete sealant—but this contraption had frozen up and begun to decay at least a century ago. Its interlinked rusted braces were clogged with fuzzy growths of moss and fungus.

Jacen squinted again, wondering why the other boy meant to salvage parts from such an old machine—but then he saw the bushy mass, a tangle of uprooted wires and cables woven together, bristling with insulation material, torn strips of cloth, and plastic. It looked almost like a. . . .

"It's a hawk-bat's nest," Zekk said. "Four eggs inside. I can see them from here, but I can't get down there by myself. If I can snatch even one of those eggs, I could sell it for enough credits to live on for a month."

"And you want *us* to help you get it?" Jaina asked.

"That's the idea," Zekk said. "Your friend Tenel Ka there has a pretty strong rope—as I found out! And some of you look like good climbers, especially that Wookiee."

Em Teedee shrilled, "Oh no, Lowbacca. You simply can*not* climb down there! I absolutely forbid it." Lowie hadn't looked too eager at first, but the translating droid's admonishment only served to convince him otherwise. The Wookiee growled an agreement to Zekk's plan.

Tenel Ka attached her grappling hook to the side of the walkway. "I am a strong climber," she said. "This is a fact."

Zekk rubbed his hands together with delight. "Excellent."

"Let me get the eggs," Jacen said, eager to touch the smooth, warm shells, to study the nest configuration. "I've always wanted to see one up close." This was such a rare opportunity. Hawk-bats were common in the deep alleyways of Coruscant, but they were horrendously difficult to capture alive.

Pulling the fibercord taut, Tenel Ka wrapped her hands around it and began lowering herself to the old construction crawler. Jacen had seen her descend the walls of the Great Temple on Yavin 4, but now he watched with renewed amazement as she walked backward down the side of the building, relying only on the strength of her supple arms and muscular legs.

Jacen admired the girl from Dathomir—

but he wished he could make her laugh. He had been telling Tenel Ka his best jokes for as long as he had known her, but he still hadn't managed to coax even the smallest smile from her. She seemed not to have a sense of humor, but he would keep trying.

Tenel Ka reached the construction crawler and anchored the fibercord, gesturing with her arm to summon him down. Jacen wrapped the cord around himself and started down the slick wall, trying to imitate Tenel Ka. He used the Force to keep his balance, nudging his feet when necessary, and soon found himself standing beside Tenel Ka on the teetering platform.

"Piece of cake," he panted, brushing his hands together.

"No, thank you," Tenel Ka said. "I am not hungry."

Jacen chuckled, but he knew the warrior girl didn't even realize she had made a joke.

Lowie slid down the fibercord with ease, while Em Teedee wailed all the way. "Oh, I can't watch! I'm switching off my optical sensors."

When they all stood on the creaking platform, Jacen bent over, straining to reach the tangled nest just below. "I'm going to climb down there," he said. "I'll pass the eggs up."

Before anyone could argue, he dropped between two thin girders, holding a crossbar to reach the piping brace that supported the odd nest. The eggs were brown, mottled with green, camouflaged as knobs of masonry covered with pale lichen. Each was about the size of Jacen's outspread hand; when he touched the warm shells, the texture was hard and rough, like rock. With the Force, he could sense the growing baby creature inside. Perhaps he could use the Force to levitate the prize up to his friends.

He smiled, tingly with wonder as he hefted one of the eggs. It wasn't heavy at all. As he touched a second egg, though, he heard a shrill shriek from above, coming closer.

Tenel Ka shouted a warning. "Look out, Jacen!"

Jacen looked up and saw the sleek form of the mother hawk-bat, swooping down at him and screaming in fury, metallic claws extended, wings studded with spikes. The hawk-bat's wingspan was about two meters. Its head consisted entirely of a horny beak with sharp ivory teeth, ready to tear a victim to shreds.

"Uh-oh," Jacen said.

Lowie bellowed in alarm. Tenel Ka grabbed

for a throwing knife—but Jacen knew he couldn't wait for help.

The creature dove toward him like a missile, and Jacen closed his eyes to reach out with the Force. His special talent had always been with animals. He could communicate with them, sense their feelings and express his own to them. "It's all right," he whispered, "I'm sorry we were invading your nest. *Calm.* It's all right. *Peace.*"

The hawk-bat pulled up from her dive and clutched one of the corroded lower crossbars with durasteel-hard claws. Jacen could hear the squeaking sound as the claws scraped rust off the metal, but he maintained his calm.

"We didn't mean to hurt your babies," he said. "We won't take them all. I need only one, and I promise you it'll be delivered to a fine and safe place . . . a beautiful zoo where it will be raised and cared for and admired by millions of people from across the galaxy."

The hawk-bat hissed and pushed her hard beak closer to Jacen, blowing foul breath from between sharp teeth. He knew the hawk-bat was extremely skeptical, but Jacen projected images of a bright aviary, a place where the young hawk-bat would be fed delicacies all its life, where it could fly freely, yet never need to fear other predators or starvation . . . or being shot at by gang members. Jacen snatched the last image—blurred figures of young humans shooting as she hunted between tall buildings—from the mother's mind.

This last feat convinced the mother, and she flapped her spiked leathery wings, backing away from the nest and leaving Jacen safe . . . for the moment. He grinned up at his friends.

Tenel Ka stood poised, dagger in hand, ready to jump down and fight. Jacen felt a pleasant warm glow to think that she was willing to defend him. He took one of the hawk-bat eggs and carefully used the Force to levitate it into Jaina's hands. She cradled it, then handed it to Zekk.

"What did you do?" Zekk called.

"I made a deal with the hawk-bat," he said. "Let's go."

"But what about those other eggs?" Zekk said, holding his treasure with great amazement.

"You only get one," Jacen answered. "That was the deal. Now we'd better get out of here—and hurry." He scrambled up to join them.

Lowie climbed the fibercord first, racing up the side of the building to the upper ledge.

Jacen urged the others to greater speed, and finally, when they were all standing back on the walkway, Zekk said, "I thought you made a deal with the mother. Why do we have to hurry?"

Jacen continued to hustle them out of sight of the construction crawler. "Because hawk-bats have extremely short memories."

ABOUT THE AUTHORS

KEVIN J. ANDERSON and his wife, **REBECCA MOESTA**, have been involved in many STAR WARS projects. Together, they are writing the six volumes of the YOUNG JEDI KNIGHTS saga for young adults, as well as creating the JUNIOR JEDI KNIGHTS series for younger readers. They are also writing a series of illustrated science books for first and second graders—the *STAR WARS* COSMIC SCIENCE series—and pop-up books showcasing the Cantina scene and the Jabba's Palace scene from the movies.

Kevin J. Anderson is also the author of the STAR WARS: JEDI ACADEMY trilogy, the forthcoming novel *Darksaber*, and the comic series DARK LORDS OF THE SITH with Tom Veitch for Dark Horse comics. His young adult fantasy novel, *Born of Elven Blood*, written with John Betancourt, was recently published by Atheneum. He has edited several STAR WARS anthologies, including *Tales From the Mos Eisley Cantina* (July 1995), in which Rebecca Moesta has a story. Rebecca Moesta will also be writing three books in the JUNIOR JEDI KNIGHTS series.